Summary

When the three spurned finalists from the TV show decide to get even and reclaim their lost fame, Blitz and Livia learn the hard way that you can quit Hollywood, but Hollywood doesn't always quit you.

Get emails or texts from Deanna about her new releases:
Deanna's List

Chapter One

I'm terribly nervous.

It's release day for the DVD set for season two of the TV reality show *Dance Blitz*.

The show is billed as *The Bachelor* meets *So You Think You Can Dance*. The star, Blitz Craven, auditions girls to be his dance partner, and possibly, his wife. He gets to pick the winner.

I wasn't supposed to be on the show.

But I charged onto the season two live finale, right as Blitz was about to announce which girl he had chosen. Rumors had been swirling that he was going to propose to one of the three finalists. Commercials and promo spots had been airing for days showing him buying a ring, smiling slyly at the camera.

He wanted to make sure the ring was perfect for "the one."

Except.

"The one" was really me.

And I wasn't even a contestant.

I knew what was really about to happen on the show. Blitz was going to do something terrible, something rash, something bad enough that he got kicked off the show, out of his obligations, and back to me.

I couldn't let that happen.

So I walked right onto the set in the middle of the live broadcast.

That is why, on this Saturday in February, I'm with Blitz as he heads toward Wild Side Tunes and TV, a music and movie superstore, to sign DVDs. Because of my crazy actions, I'm part of his fame. We're a package deal.

It's the weekend before Valentine's Day, and Blitz's manager Hannah is positive that our being together on this promotional tour is going to send DVD sales into the stratosphere. Blitz and I don't care about that. But she does. And the lawyers who drew up Blitz's contract do.

So here we are in LA.

Blitz takes my hand. We're in a limo because, of course, we have to be, driving up to a store where apparently over a thousand screaming fans have been standing in line since yesterday to ensure they got a chance to see Blitz.

We have to look the part of Reality TV Royalty, whatever that is. Hannah talks really fast, and I generally only catch every tenth word, the ones she says more emphatically, like they're in bold uppercase letters.

And **REALITY TV ROYALTY** is definitely a phrase she emphasizes.

The words make me think of mostly negative things. I missed four years of television due to my father's iron rule, but in the two months since I left home, I've caught up on some of the big shows. *Dance Moms. Hoarders. Real Housewives.*

If they are royalty, I'm not sure I want the throne.

"Your dress is killing me," Blitz says. "I'm never going to make it through hours of signing without stealing you away."

I glance down. The dress isn't anything I would have picked out, but Hannah and her wardrobe people descended on us in the hotel, fitting me into everything from jeans and slashed leather vests to glittery ball gowns.

Nobody asked my opinion. In the end, they chose a stretchy dance outfit like you might see an ice-skater wear. It isn't too crazy, the sparkly emerald skirt reaching halfway down my thigh. The fit is more demure than some of the things they've put on me.

But it does have diamond-shaped cutouts. One shows a lot of cleavage, and another one reveals my belly button. I was too paranoid to even eat breakfast, afraid any bit of roundness to my middle would lead to screaming tabloid headlines about a baby bump.

I get a little sensitive when people talk about babies.

Blitz looks exactly like they always have him dressed on the show. Sleek black jazz pants. A silk shirt in a pale mint green that complements my dress perfectly.

His black hair is short again, cut a few days ago by the original hairdresser from *Dance Blitz*. And the sexy stubble on his face is trimmed the way I've always known it. I reach up to run my fingers along his jaw. We are in this together.

He kisses my fingers. "Are we almost there?"

"Oh, for heaven's sake, check Google," Hannah says with irritation. She holds a compact mirror up, trying to apply lipstick on the bumpy drive.

I don't know why she's annoyed, or why she's adding lipstick right now. She looks perfectly put together already. She wears a mossy gray-green suit with a pencil skirt, which I realize totally matches me and Blitz.

I'm sure some marketing research has told her that this is what will make her look like she is in charge of us. She wants to ensure that everyone around us asks *her* what to do, not us.

That's what she does.

Blitz closes his eyes and holds my hand to his cheek. I know he doesn't want to do this publicity stop. We've put our *Dance Blitz* days behind us. He's confident that we can simply buy a house in San Antonio, where real estate is cheap compared to LA, and live comfortably forever on what he's already earned.

With Dreamcatcher Dance Academy training us, life is perfect. I get to see my birth daughter Gabriella in ballet class. Her adoptive mother still doesn't know who I am. No one does but Blitz. Our secret has remained safe despite the publicity.

We see no need to change anything. This DVD signing is the end of our public spotlight.

The driver rolls down the window separating the front seat from the back section of the limo. "We're about to approach," he says.

Hannah turns to him. "Don't get out to open the door. We have security waiting who will keep the crowd back as Blitz and Livia enter the building. You'll drive me around the rear for a quieter entrance."

The driver nods.

"I miss Ted," I say. He's a high school friend of

Blitz's who served as my driver and bodyguard back in San Antonio.

"We can bring him out to LA if you want," Blitz says.

"That's okay. We're only here for a couple more days."

Hannah snaps her mirror shut. "What happened to Duke? I'm surprised you didn't want him managing security for this event."

Blitz shrugs. "I haven't talked to him since everything went down."

I squeeze Blitz's hand. He doesn't want to make any more than a passing reference to his mega-downfall, where he Tweeted a naked picture of one of the finalists along with a really terrible comment about her. The Tweet went viral and got him kicked off his own show for months. It's how we met.

Hannah frowns. She picks up her phone and taps a button. "Lisa, check Duke Riordan's employment status with Blitz's estate. He's not doing any duties currently."

She sets down the phone. "Does he still have access to security?"

Blitz sighs. "I have no idea. I haven't been to my LA condo since I left town last October."

Hannah presses her perfectly lined coral lips together. "That was five months ago! And you've been paying him, probably to sneak around your place and collect things to sell on eBay. I say bring him back on board or take him off the payroll. It's high time you got your act together."

"You think there are still cameras all over your old house?" I ask.

"I'm sure there are," Blitz says. "I don't even know how to go about finding them all. Half were hidden behind mirrors or in plants."

"There are services for that," Hannah says. "But you're still obligated to keep them until the end of your contract."

"You're still under contract for the show?" I ask.

"That's why we're here," Blitz says.

Hannah looks from me to Blitz and back again. "You two remind everyone what true love looks like, and this will go fine. You're a team, remember?"

"We're a team," I say, and move our clasped hands over to my cheek this time. "This will be fun, right?"

Blitz grunts. I look away from Hannah's smirk.

We turn the corner and the limo is spotted by the fans lined up around the side of a two-story glass and steel building. The screams begin, so loud and piercing that they penetrate to the interior.

"Whoa," I say.

"I can tell you right now," Blitz says to Hannah, his voice low and threatening, "that there is not enough security on that line."

"You should have called Duke," Hannah says

dryly. "I hired a very established company, but he knows your fans." She glances out the window. "They are rather ardent."

Girls are standing all around the block, holding signs, hugging each other, crying, yelling, and jumping up and down as we roll by. One lifts her shirt and tries to run to the car, bare boobs bouncing. A friend pulls her back.

My face flushes hot. Do girls always do that? I glance at Blitz, but he's not paying any attention to the crowd, staring out the opposite window.

"Well, this is a lark," Hannah says, her voice dripping with sarcasm. "Bad boys bring out the worst in them."

"He's not a bad boy anymore," I say.

"Tell that to them," Hannah says. "They're binge-watching all his clips. The media he has built up will never die. They'll still think he's a hot, young woman-izing heartbreaker when he's sixty-five."

Blitz laughs. "That's fine. They're never going to see me get old."

Hannah smooths her skirt. "I'm sure you'll do more television work."

"Don't count on it," Blitz says. He pulls me close. "I'm going to dance with this girl, teach wheelchair ballerinas, and enjoy my obscurity."

"Sounds like you're putting me out of a job," Hannah says.

Blitz doesn't answer as we pull up to the front of the store. Waist-high wooden barricades keep the fans back, and two security men with broad shoulders hold out their arms as the girls threaten to spill over the walls.

A third man opens our car door. The screams are deafening.

"Let's do this," Blitz says, although I see his lips move more than I actually hear him. The noise is intense.

We duck as we cross the limo to the door. I'm not a drinker, but the sparkling decanter resting in the side bar looks rather inviting as we face this onslaught of fans.

Blitz tucks my hand under his arm and steps out.

I didn't think it was possible for the noise to get louder, but it does.

He turns and leads me out of the car. I expect everyone to go silent, upset at the evidence that Blitz is taken. But, unbelievably, the screams go up another notch.

At first all the insanity seems to be about Blitz. They wear T-shirts with his face and hold hand-lettered signs, their cell phones all taking video.

Then I spot four girls in pale blue dresses on the opposite side. They are all wearing black wigs. "Blitz!" I yell. "Are they dressed as me?"

"Look at that!" he says. He walks right over to them, and they all start screaming.

Blitz waves at me, still frozen by the limo. "Come here and take a picture!" he yells.

I move toward them with hesitation. I've never had anything like this happen. I couldn't even have imagined it.

Blitz pulls out his own cell phone, and the screaming behind the blue-dress girls reaches a fever pitch.

"Selfie mode!" Blitz says, holding the phone high and pulling me against him next to the girls. Once he's taken the shot, he tells them, "I'll post this to my Twitter feed later so you can have it. Love the dresses."

I think one of them is going to faint. As we head into the door of the DVD shop, two of the girls are crying and shouting, "We love you, Livia!" over and over again.

I want to turn around and take it all in, really look at these fans. They are so passionate about Blitz, and I guess, some of them, about me. I catch sight of one more sign that says "Livia spells C-O-U-R-A-G-E."

The man who opened the car door stands by the entrance to the store. "This way," he says.

I follow Blitz in, feeling starstruck in reverse. How is this happening? They can't be interested in me, a two-year ballet student who can barely hold *en pointe*.

A small group of employees in red Wild Side shirts, plus a man in a horribly loud cherry suit, wait for us just inside. When the door closes, the quiet is bliss.

"You have quite a lot of fans out there," the man says. "I'm Lewis, owner of Wild Side Tunes and TV." He reaches to shake Blitz's hand. "We are delighted to have you here today."

Lewis reminds me of the used-car salesmen I used to see on TV ads. But he seems friendly. He introduces four employees who will be helping organize the line and keep things moving. We follow Lewis as we cut through shelves of movies and CDs to a set of stairs.

"We'll control access to you via the stairs," Lewis says, pointing up. "Fans will go up these, cross to you at a table up there, and then come down the other side."

Hannah walks up from the back of the store as he's finishing. "I assume you have an emergency exit in case of a rush?" she asks. "We need a safety plan."

"Freight elevator is directly to the right of the signing table," Lewis says. "We have six security guards. My staff will brief you on the situation. Former presidents have held public events here. We have it covered."

Hannah nods.

"There is a private room where you two can wait until we begin," Lewis says. "About fifteen minutes until we open the doors."

I turn back to the windows. "Can we see outside from up there?" I ask.

"Yes," Lewis says. "It's a nice view of the street. Would you rather wait there?"

"Yes," I say. "I want to see everything."

Blitz steps aside and gestures to the stairs. "Lead the way, my lady. I'll follow you anywhere."

We head up, Lewis behind us. Hannah and the staff have moved elsewhere.

The front of the store is all glass, so when we reach the second floor and look out, all the fans piled up outside can see us. Most are in an orderly row that snakes around the building, but others are clumped together on the sidewalk outside the doors.

"We've given away three hundred wristbands to the ones we think you can get to during your allotted time. We estimate there are about eight hundred more who won't get in," Lewis says.

"That's terrible!" I say. "They wait all night and don't even get in!" I turn to Blitz. "That isn't fair!"

"It's part of the deal," Blitz says. "We can only sign so fast."

"We'll have to be faster!" I say.

Blitz puts his arm around me. As we stand at

the rail overlooking the store and the crowd outside, I start to actually feel a little like royalty. I lift my hand to wave at everyone, and the sudden increase in volume is audible even from inside.

A girl in a red shirt approaches. "Ten minutes, sir. We have six media representatives downstairs asking to set up. What should I do with them?"

"I'll handle it," Lewis says. He turns to us. "I'll confer with your manager about the press. Enjoy your last quiet moments. Sharon, can you show them where the private bathroom is and what the plan will be should they need a break?"

Sharon nods. "This way," she says.

I'm impressed by her laid-back manner around Blitz. She acts like he is any customer. Maybe that's why she has this particular job. She isn't impressed by fame.

Sharon shows us the table, the path to the bathroom, and talks about the security that will be at the tables. Then another girl in a red shirt races up the stairs.

"Don't let them go to the bathroom alone!" she says, huffing from her dash. "His manager says to keep them apart."

Blitz and I look at each other for a second as Sharon's face blooms red. Then he laughs, so hard and so long that I can't help but join him.

"Challenge accepted," he says, and pulls on my hand to take me to the bathroom.

The other girl panics, trying to block our way. "Your manager says you will destroy her hair and makeup."

"I like it when he does that," I say.

She looks horror stricken, as if she will be personally held responsible if I have an eyelash out of place.

Blitz lets her off the hook. "Don't worry about it. We don't have any plans to deflower your private bathroom's innocence."

"We don't?" I ask, and both girls' faces match their shirts.

"Oh, now I'm tempted." Blitz leans in to kiss me when Hannah's sharp "Don't you dare mess up her lipstick!" temporarily stops him.

"Oh, but I will," he whispers, and lightly brushes his lips against mine. It's not enough to do any damage.

Then he releases me and says, "Hannah, you spoil all the fun at these things."

Hannah is indignant. "Blitz Craven, I've defended your manhandling of enough dancers to last a lifetime. But you'll save it for the cameras and at least let us get some proper publicity shots before you muck everything up." Hannah's face is set, her posture in the green outfit like that of an angry schoolteacher.

Feet thunder on the stairs. I half expect the fans

to be invading, but it's just an army of photographers, camera crews, and at least two reporters holding microphones. I feel my panic closing in. Nobody said we'd have to talk to the cameras! I thought this was just a signing, fans would come and go and snap pictures, and then we'd be done! I clutch at Blitz's hand.

"You have five until we open the doors," Lewis says.

"Nonsense," Hannah cuts in. "We'll get what we need before we let them in."

Lewis gives her a quick nod. "Whatever the lady wants."

"Blitz?" I whisper. "What is this?" I turn my back to the people setting up lights and camera stands.

"It'll be fine," he says. "You don't have to say anything."

"Nobody prepped me for interviews! Nobody told me what to say!"

Blitz holds my cheeks with both palms and looks me straight in the eyes. "You are fine. Nobody coaches us. Just speak from your heart."

"What if my heart wants to set them on fire?"

Blitz gives a throaty laugh and pulls me against him. "You're too perfect, Princess," he says. Flashes start to pop.

Hannah walks by us and says in a low singsong voice, "Don't muss her makeup!"

Blitz twirls a curl of my hair. I want to hide in him, bury my face against his strong chest. But we're not alone anymore. We're in front of the people who can make or break us. And they're probably already recording. For all I know, this is live on some online feed.

"You can do it," Blitz says.

I take a deep breath. I was brave enough to walk unannounced on live TV, I can smile in front of a few cameras.

One of the women is already recording in front of a giant sign that reads "*Dance Blitz*."

She says into the camera, "We're here with Blitz Craven and his surprise contestant at the signing of the DVDs for *Dance Blitz*. The intense season ended with the dancing Romeo's newest lover storming onstage to seize the title from the three finalists who had been working all season to woo the man of their dreams."

I spot the red light on the camera that is trained on her.

And the panic starts to take over.

I am so not up for this.

Chapter Two

❧

"My parents might see this," I whisper to Blitz as the reporter stops the recording and repeats it all again. She's obviously not live.

"And what will they do?" Blitz asks. "Ground you?" He walks us over to the table, a little farther from the cameramen setting up lights and tripods. "You're with me now. They don't control you."

"But if everyone finds out who they are, people might camp out at their house and ask them questions," I say.

He kisses my hand for the hundredth time that day. "Livia, nobody bothers my parents. Remember at the city jail a few weeks ago, picking up Baby Daddy? Nobody even recognized my dad."

He's right. Maybe nobody really cares about my family.

"Besides," Blitz says, "we've given them a fake last name for you. With no social media footprint, and no connections to anyone, they can't find you. Nobody knows where you came from."

He's right. Hannah came up with Livia Mays, close enough to my real name that I wouldn't screw it up if someone used it, but common enough to be generic. For the first time, I'm glad I was home-schooled. There is literally nothing on the Internet anywhere with my real name or picture. Nobody knows me. There's no glib classmates to interview, no high school teachers to say what I was like.

Although due to Gabriella, there are definitely secrets to dig up. Big ones.

My confidence falters again.

Hannah claps her hands. "Douglas," she says, smiling at one of the reporters, "why don't you place Livia and Blitz where you would like them, and we can start?"

Blitz and I glance at each other. Hannah never gives up control of these things. She must think this guy is important.

A friendly man in a shiny gray suit that looks like it came off a runway model, almost too short in the legs, pencil thin, and close fitted, hurries forward and extends his hand. "Blitz, Livia, delighted to be here today. I appreciate this opportunity to talk with you both."

I shake his hand weakly.

"Hey, Doug," Blitz says, "I hear you're short-listed for the new entertainment hour."

"That I am," Doug says. "Decision on that should be announced any day."

I can tell from Blitz's subtle reluctance that he thinks this Doug guy is going to do something dramatic to increase his chances of getting whatever show this is. He's wary, so of course I'm panicked. Even more than before.

Hannah watches from a distance, a pleased expression on her face, like she's a cat that just got the dog sent outside in the rain.

My anxiety makes me feel hot. I touch my fingertips to my hairline, where I might be starting to sweat. I'm more likely to destroy my makeup than Blitz at this point.

Doug gestures to a couple of armchairs situated at the end of the rows of books behind the tables where we're signing. "Let's head over here."

Without Doug saying a word, a girl in a black shirt shoves a third armchair over to the first pair. The other cameramen and reporters seem annoyed as Doug commandeers the situation. Another girl clips tiny silver microphones to my dress and Blitz's shirt.

"Is this an exclusive?" asks the female reporter who recorded her intro. "Because nobody told me this was exclusive."

"Of course not," Doug says. "You guys can cut in anytime."

But his chair is close enough that it's probably hard to keep him out of the shot. And I'm pretty sure the woman won't want Doug's voice in her recording.

The tension between them is intense. Blitz leans forward in his chair, his elbows on his knees. "Doug, maybe you can ask a few questions, and then we'll move on to..." he hesitates, looking at the woman expectantly.

"Geneva," the woman says with an edge in her voice. "Geneva Farmington from the local affiliate."

"Thanks for being here, Geneva," Blitz says. He flashes her one of his megawatt smiles and she melts a little.

I'm not annoyed by this. I know it's one of his tactics. He has them for men too. He's very good at sizing up a person and delivering the right dose of attitude or charm.

Doug nods knowingly. "Always good to keep the locals happy," he says. "Of course, mine is a national broadcast."

"A *cable* broadcast," Geneva fires back. "National *networks* will pick up mine."

Blitz doesn't really seem up for moderating them. He glances at Hannah. Normally she would be all over this like she was with the store owner, but for some reason, she's perfectly happy to sit back and let the situation unfold.

"Let's get going," Blitz says. "I don't really like making the fans wait."

The thick round arms of the upholstered chairs keep me and Blitz separate. We can't easily reach each other to so much as hold hands.

"So what are your plans for the three unfinished bonus episodes?" Doug asks. "Since this lovely lady took over the job of the contestants, will we be meeting her family and watching you two plan a wedding?"

Blitz's expression gets hard. "Livia is not part of the deal, Doug," he says. "And as far as I'm concerned, those three episodes are digital smoke."

"What do you think, Livia?" Doug asks. "Are you ready for Blitz to meet your family?"

I glance at Blitz. "Not on camera," I say shakily. "I don't think they've agreed to that."

Doug laughs. "I doubt it. Were you ready for the load of fame that came with Blitz?"

Blitz jumps in. "We're working on our dancing together," he says. "We've only just started to figure out our personal style."

Doug flashes a knowing grin. "You just said 'our.' Are there wedding plans on the horizon?"

I can see when Blitz settles in and decides to pour out the charm. He sits back in the chair, lacing his fingers together behind his head. This is the Blitz I remember from watching talk show clips before I knew him.

"I imagine Livia has a say in that," he says. "I figure I better show her I'm not a carousing schmuck. Tall order."

The two men laugh. Blitz has Doug's number. Now he'll feed him what he needs to get this over and done.

I hold my hands together tightly, sitting tall, mostly anxious that my skirt is short enough that I might give the cameras a crotch shot. My thighs ache from holding my knees together.

"How about those three lovelies from the show?" Doug asks. "Have you heard from them? Did they seem upset about the outcome?"

Blitz flashes a smile. "You'll have to talk to my lawyers about that one, Doug. You know women."

My face flames a bit at this one. I glance over at Hannah to see if Blitz is behaving the way she wants. Her arms are crossed, a twisted smile on her face. She sees me looking at her, and moves her fingers to the corners of her mouth to remind me to smile.

Uggh. I plaster one on and turn back to Blitz. When he sees me, his expression shifts, like he realizes he's fallen into his old pattern. He sits forward again and reaches over the top of the two chair arms to find my hand.

"Are you quite through, Doug?" Geneva stands just off camera, her microphone in her hand.

Doug glances at Hannah, and I feel Blitz stiffen, his hand on mine painfully tight. I turn my attention to him, wondering what is going on.

And that's when I see them.

All three of them, dressed in flashy dresses, tons of cleavage, model-perfect hair, strolling in like they are the horsemen from the apocalypse.

The angry dethroned finalists from *Dance Blitz*.

Chapter Three

B litz jumps from his chair. "This was a setup!"

Giselle smirks and juts her hips. Her honey-red hair is pale and lovely, falling around her face like Jessica Rabbit. Her red dress must be taped to her body, because the deep V plunges to her waist but molds to her curves. I feel dowdy just looking at her.

"Blitz, baby," she says. "I really hope you didn't think you were done with us."

She sidles up to the chair. "Cameras are rolling, darling," she says, her hands on Blitz's shoulders. "Sit a spell."

Blitz falls back into the chair. Giselle sits on the arm next to him.

Mariah, the dark-haired finalist, looks as regal as a princess in a cobalt blue dress slit up her thigh. She walks behind Blitz and perches on the back.

Christy has totally changed her look, sweet and girl-next-door in a pretty pale yellow sundress. You would never guess that fans had once called her a "skank." They've gotten organized. Stylists and coaches.

Christy curls up at his feet. The four of them look ready for a photo shoot, the image perfectly balanced.

Planned. Every bit of it.

And Blitz knows. He tries to stand up again, but this time all three girls put their hands on him and push him back in place.

"Smile for us, Blitz honey," Giselle says through her teeth as the cameras flash. "You're about to go viral."

I realize I've shrunk away from the group, scooting to the far side of my chair. My brain feels erased, and I'm paralyzed. Who did this?

Flashes start popping. I turn to Hannah to see if it was her or this Doug guy, and she stands with her arms crossed, looking very satisfied.

Oh, she is so fired. If there is any way we can get rid of her, we will do it.

"So, ladies, how does it feel to be back with Blitz?" Doug asks.

"Oh, we weren't near through with this boy," Giselle purrs. She runs a hand through Blitz's hair and I want to slap her arm right off him.

Blitz looks about to explode. He notices Hannah's posture as well, and the cameras. Then he steals a glance at me.

I'm sure I look like a scared rabbit. He closes his eyes a moment, then turns to Doug. "It seems some people won't take no for an answer."

The girls giggle.

I manage to straighten my spine and sit more normally in the chair. "Lewis?" I say, not really sure where my own voice is coming from.

The store owner pops out from behind the camera crew. "Yes, Livia?" he asks.

"Isn't it time to let the fans up?"

"Past time," he says.

"And how many girls out there are dressed as them?" I wave my hand in the general direction of the finalists.

Lewis smiles. "Why, I don't believe I saw any."

Hannah's smile has faded and now a calculating look is on her face. She's underestimated me.

"Can you let the Livias in first?" I ask. "They seemed to be near the front. As a special favor."

"I'd be delighted," Lewis says. He motions to one of the employees. "It does sound as though we should adjourn this interview and move to the signing table."

He comes forward to take my hand and lift me from the chair, blocking the cameras from their view of me.

Blitz jumps from his seat, avoiding the three girls. He takes my hand and we head over to the signing table, where there are just two padded folding chairs.

"I think those girls have had their say," I tell Lewis. "You said you had some security?"

"I do," he says with a wink.

Two of the burly guards head over to the finalists. I make a point not to watch what happens, organizing the pens and water bottles in front of us.

Blitz stares over at his manager as if he could shoot poison darts from his eyes. We're more or less alone, the photographers packing up now that we're in less interesting positions and the flamboyant girls are gone. Geneva talks with Doug in hushed angry tones.

"You okay?" I ask Blitz. I know how I'm feeling, scared to death and shocked that I was able to say what I did. My hands are trembling still.

"I'm fine," he says. "You were brilliant and got Lewis on your side. Cut those she-devils off at the knees by stopping their publicity." He finally lets his eyes rest on me. "I haven't been in charge of my own career since *Dance Blitz* started," he says. "Everyone else has always run it, and I've done what was expected of me."

"I know," I say. "It's hard. Contracts and all."

"Screw the contracts," Blitz says. "Let them sue me. I'm not going to do anything with those women."

DEANNA ROY

The blue-dress girls start making their way up the stairs, followed by the snaking line. The noise levels rise dramatically as the first segments of the crowd are allowed inside the store.

Blitz looks at them and smiles. "You always surprise me, Livia. You seem so shy and unassuming. Then you walk onto live television and make me dance with you. Or you take total charge of a press interview."

Lewis holds the crowd for another moment, checking wristbands and waving over two employees with large boxes of DVDs.

"You taught me that," I say to Blitz, leaning over to kiss his cheek. A flash pops and I realize the cameras haven't really retreated, just moved back. "We're going to make this work. Nobody can make you do anything."

The line moves forward and the blue-dress girls dash to the table. Blitz and I greet them and start our rhythm of pictures, signing, and smiles.

Blitz calls Geneva over and gives her an exclusive interview with us and the Livia fans.

But his manager Hannah stays off to one side, sitting in one of the round chairs we vacated. She watches us with an intensity that makes me squirm. I know if she has her way, Blitz won't have that chance to drop into obscurity like he wants.

And now she knows that I actually do stand in her way.

Chapter Four

When the signing finally ends, we load into the limo with a sour-faced Hannah.

We're less than a mile from the DVD store when the limo rolls to a stop.

Hannah turns to the driver. "What are you doing?"

"He's doing what I asked," Blitz says. "And *we* are getting away from you as fast as possible." Blitz flings the back door open. "You don't set up your biggest client like that and expect him to be all gracious and thankful."

Hannah's coral lips pinch together. "You have a contract meeting at the set in three hours," she says. "Don't be late."

Blitz helps me out of the limo, then peers back in

at her. "I'll be there, Hannah. Unlike my manager, I respect the people I work with."

He slams the door.

The limo driver escorts us over to a Mercedes, driven by yet another driver, this one younger and casually dressed in jeans and a white shirt.

"Right on," he says and opens the door for us.

I glance back. Thankfully, Hannah hasn't come out of the limo.

We load into the new car and Blitz greets the new driver. "We're starving," he says. "Can you take us somewhere between here and the studio?"

"Sure. You want something fancy? Or casual?"

"Casual," Blitz says. "Livia, what are you hungry for?"

I glance down at the diamond cutout of my dress. I should have brought a change of clothes. "A salad?"

"You're right," Blitz says. "I love that outfit, but I'm sure you want out of it." He picks up his phone and hits a button. "Actually just take us to the Apple Pan," he says to the driver. "Scout the inside."

The driver nods. Then Blitz is on his phone. "Jerry, run to my room and fetch outfits for me and Livia. Jeans and plain stuff." He looks over at me for confirmation and I nod. He glances down at my feet. "And some shoes. You have good taste. Bring it to the Apple Pan or just send it in a car."

Jerry is one of the wardrobe people. Probably the only one I like.

Blitz sticks his phone in his pocket. "We're going to be hot stuff for the next day or two after that footage gets out, but I think we'll be okay for a few hours. You have sunglasses?"

I dig in my bag and pull out a pair.

"I don't want you walking around in that dress. Images are probably already all over of it, and you'll very easily be spotted."

I glance down again. It is a stupidly recognizable dress, bright green and revealing.

"Come here," Blitz says. He pulls me against him. "Have I told you lately that you are incredible?"

I shake my head against his shoulder.

"Well, you are."

"Should I go back to the hotel after we eat?" I ask.

"Bennett asked for you to be at the contract meeting," Blitz says.

I sit up straight. "Bennett will be here?" He's the benefactor behind Dreamcatcher Dance Academy, and he personally flew me to LA to be on Blitz's show. It was his wife's idea.

"Yes. He's a producer and he knew you'd be more comfortable with him there."

"Why am I involved?" I ask. "I didn't sign anything."

"You were on the show," Blitz says. "Hannah is treating us like a package deal."

"Then why did she have the finalists ambush us at a signing?"

He shakes his head. "I have no idea. I'm sure we're going to find out this afternoon."

"Are there always contract meetings on weekends?"

"Hollywood doesn't work on a normal schedule," Blitz says. "The industry is your life."

"Interesting timing, though," I say.

"Isn't it?" Blitz says. "Makes you wonder what they have up their sleeves."

We pull up in front of a rather simple white building with green pillars. "What is this place?" I ask.

"A diner," Blitz says. "I'm going to have every type of pie."

"Pie," I say wistfully. "Now that's something I haven't had in a while."

"We are going to eat so much pie," he says.

The driver parks around the corner. "Doesn't look too crazy," he says. "Let me go check the situation."

Blitz nods.

We sit snuggled against each other on the leather seat. I feel my anxiety levels start to drop a little. "I guess we should have brought a change of clothes," I say. "Now we have to wait on Jerry."

"It's fine," he says. "I just wanted away from Hannah, and I'm sure she went back to the hotel."

"Can you fire her?"

"Sure, but there's a hell of a kill fee for her. And she still gets a percentage of anything related to *Dance Blitz*. She covered her ass."

"Was she different when you hired her?" I ask.

Blitz laughs. "You don't hire Hannah. She chooses you. You don't say no to her."

"Does she have other clients?"

"Not currently. She drops them if they aren't performing. If I'm lucky, she'll dump me."

"Sounds like she has plans to keep you working." I watch Blitz's face as his eyebrows draw together in annoyance.

"She knows I can cut and run. They will all play their hand at the meeting later."

The driver returns to his seat. "They've reserved two chairs at the far side of the bar whenever you're ready."

"Thanks," Blitz says. "We just need Jerry."

"He shouldn't be far behind unless he's slow to leave," the driver says. "The hotel is closer to here than we were."

"Jerry can be indecisive," Blitz says.

"Isn't that him?" I ask.

A wiry man in familiar rectangular glasses gets out

of a car down the street. "I'll flag him," the driver says.

We watch as they exchange a leather bag.

Then the back door opens and the driver hands it to me. "I can escort you to the bathroom if you like."

"I really don't want to be seen in this," I say.

"The windows are dark," Blitz says. "Just leave us to it."

The driver shuts the door and discreetly walks half a block down.

"You sure?" I ask. He's right about the back windows, but the front window is clear.

"I'm not going to let anyone get even the smallest look." He turns and props himself between the two front seats, effectively blocking anyone's view through the car from the windshield. "Except me, of course. I'm going to stare like a dying man."

"You're terrible," I say, unzipping the bag. Inside is a soft white short-sleeved sweater and my favorite Juicy Couture jeans. "Jerry is a miracle," I say.

"Your naked body is a miracle," Blitz says. "Now let me see it."

I slip off a shoe and toss it at him. He laughs as he catches it.

I'm not shy with Blitz, but we are in a car on an open street and I know what I'm wearing beneath this dress. That is to say, not much.

The diamond cutouts mean no bra, just built-in

padding, and only a tiny string thong, low slung to avoid cutting across the belly opening.

I carefully lay out the clothes on the seat so I can grab them quickly.

I get the dress up and over my face when it catches for a second on my hair. Blitz sucks in a breath. "Oh, if I dared to take a picture of this," he says.

"You learned your lesson on that," I say, trying to pull the dress off, but several sequins have caught in my wild curls.

"Hold on a second," he says, and moves forward. More light comes from the windshield.

"Stop!" I say. "People will see in!"

Blitz moves back into position. "Then I'll just stay here and enjoy the show."

My arms are still in the tight sleeves, the dress caught in my hair. Otherwise, I'm almost completely naked, only the whisper-thin straps of the thong leading to the smallest triangle of fabric imaginable.

My fingers work to sort out where the worst of the tangle is between my hair and the sparkly bodice of the dress. I'm not particularly well endowed, but I'm jerking hard enough that my breasts sway a little as I try to get free.

"God, I'm not going to be able to go out in public for a year with this hard-on," Blitz says.

"I've almost got it," I say.

"Take your time," Blitz says.

Finally, no doubt with a solid swath of my hair, the dress comes free. I toss the silly thing on the floor.

"Oh, just like that, right there," Blitz says. His eyes are on my body.

"Blitz!" I frantically look out the side window. There's no one on the street, thankfully, although I know the tint is dark enough for our privacy.

"If we were in a limo, we would so not be going in for pie," Blitz says. He reaches forward and slides his fingers along my collarbone, down a breast, and across my belly. For the barest second, he delves between my thighs.

It's intoxicating to have him sitting there, his hands on my body. Thousands of girls were dying to fling themselves at him all morning, but he's here in this car with me.

My heart races, the hot thudding between my legs impossible to ignore. I wonder what we could get away with in here, what I'm brave enough to do.

Blitz senses my hesitation and raises his eyebrow as he says, "Three more seconds and my face is going to be between your legs."

A horn honks outside and a car slows down for a woman walking a dog across the street just ahead of us. I let out a little "Oh!" and dive to the floorboard, crossing my arms over my body.

Blitz laughs. "Here's your sweater, Princess," he says, passing it to me.

I don't care that I don't have a bra on. The sweater is fuzzy and will hide me. I jerk it over my head.

"So close," Blitz says. "I almost had you."

I reach over for the jeans and plop onto the seat, pulling them on as fast as possible. Only when they are zipped and snapped do I calm down.

Blitz moves back to his seat. "This is going to take a while to settle down." He gestures to his crotch in the satiny jazz pants. It's bulging out rather spectacularly.

"I thought you wanted pie," I say demurely.

"To hell with pie," he says, but he pulls his own jeans out of the bag.

When we're both put together, Blitz in his hat and shades, and me with my hair in enough order to pass muster, we get out of the car.

The driver walks a little ahead, watching for anyone who might spot us. We enter the diner, which has red chairs lining a bar that surrounds a red-brick work area with cooks in white hats.

I hold on to Blitz's hand and whisper, "This place is amazing!"

"Wait till you try the pie," he says.

The chairs are full other than two on the far side,

tucked near the wall. We take them and pick up a laminated menu.

"Just get one of everything," I say. "I'm not wearing those stupid cutouts anymore."

"You have no idea what I wanted to do to those cutouts," Blitz says.

"Oh, I can probably figure it out." We grin foolishly at each other behind the oversized menus, and I'm struck with the similarity to the scene in the movie *Grease*. I saw it so long ago, before movies were banned at home.

Blitz orders a pair of burgers and all three of their signature pies. By the time we eat it all and stumble outside, I'm doubly glad I'm not in the green dress anymore. My belly bump is a food baby.

"I guess it's on to the studio now," Blitz says.

"Aren't we early?" I ask.

"Yeah, but it might be fun to look around. I don't think you saw much of it when you were on the show."

"Just the dressing room, some viewing room, and backstage," I say.

"Oh, there's lots of fun places." He leans forward. "Let's head on over," he says to the driver.

I'm excited to be headed back to the studio where I first changed my life for Blitz.

Just like last time, I have no idea what might be in store for us there.

Chapter Five

B litz takes my hand as he leads me down the hall
I remember from the finale. But then it was
bustling with people, crew members and dancers.
Now the rooms are all eerily quiet.

"You probably were in here," Blitz says, tapping
his knuckles on the door at the corner. He's right,
that was the room where everyone watched the show
on mounted televisions. "It's a viewing room."

"Yes," I say. "And a couple doors down was where
the makeup artists were set up."

Blitz knocks against that one as well as we pass.
"I've never been in there," he says.

"You have your own makeup person, then?"
I ask.

"Yes, and my own dressing room."

"I didn't see it that night," I say, but thinking over

the episodes of *Dance Blitz*, I could remember scenes that took place there.

And some of the girls who snuck in.

I shove those thoughts away. "Are we going to it?" I ask.

"I'll take you in if you like. It's on the other side."

He must see my frown, because he quickly adds, "It's not important, though. And yeah, there were always lots of cameras in it."

"Which girl took a bet from the others to try and catch you naked?" I ask, trying to sound as if none of that really matters. And it doesn't, I guess. It's his past. But still. The antics on the show are hard to watch now.

"I don't remember her name," Blitz says. "Was it season one?"

"I think so," I say, glad the girl doesn't stick in his mind. "She found you, though."

"Yeah," Blitz says. "It was scripted. I was literally in there freezing my ass off while she tried to be all ninja. The cameraman in the corner was giving me a countdown for when she'd arrive."

"She was only wearing a towel," I say.

"Also scripted. I think she was supposed to be pretending she was lost."

"Everybody could see it was fake."

"I'm sure." Blitz grasps my hand. "Most of the show was fake."

"Did you really have sex with her? The show makes it look like you did, right there with the cameras."

He sighs. "I wasn't in it to be subtle," he says.

He didn't answer the question.

It doesn't matter. I have to keep reminding myself of that.

But there's a little tension between us as we walk these halls. This was his space with all those girls.

The articles written about Blitz during the show say that twenty of the fifty contestants confirmed sleeping with him, sometimes more than one of them on the same day. But who knows? That was just what they would say to get headlines and airtime. I see how it works now.

I squeeze his hand. I can't let his wild past impact how we are now.

We pass the doors to backstage. I pause, looking up at the red and green "on air" lights above the sign that reads STUDIO A. It's all dark right now. "It was so wild to see you out there, and the audience. It was surreal," I say.

"I can't believe you did it. More than one contestant has frozen up when they stepped out."

"Really?"

"Yeah, especially in season one. Two got eliminated over it. Only one girl got a dramatic story line about her stage fright."

"Yes, I remember. The tall one."

"Farrah," Blitz says. "I really felt for her and tried to help her. But something about that camera light turning on would just freak her out."

"Poor thing."

Blitz keys in a code on the door and it pops open. "Let's go in."

It's pitch black beyond the door, although when my eyes adjust, I can make out the pale glow of emergency lighting along parts of the floor.

Blitz flips a switch and red light bathes the backstage. I can make out some of the equipment and props, waiting for a season that will never come.

"When will they clear all this out?" I ask.

Blitz shrugs. "I'm guessing we're about to negotiate someone else taking over. It can be like *The Bachelor*, where a new dancer auditions new contestants every season."

"But you're the Blitz of *Dance Blitz*," I say.

"Maybe they want me to make appearances," he says. "Based on today, I'm not sure I'm willing to negotiate even that."

We wander closer to the stage, which is lined with emergency lights, presumably so nobody falls off in the dark. It's a solid eight-foot drop to the floor if you don't take the side stairs. The seats for the audience are set on risers.

The stage is completely bare. Blitz changes his

grip on my hand and twirls me out. My hair flies as I reach the end of his arm and reverse back up against him.

"It all started right here," he says.

"The end of the beginning," I say.

He slips his arm around my waist. "True. We went from secret couple to public spectacle in a single dance."

We cross to the other side of the stage. I didn't ever venture this way the night I stormed onto the show. On this side, props are everywhere, stacked tightly against each other. We have to carve a way through them in the near-dark.

I bump against a lamppost. "I remember that one," I say.

"These are mostly from the finale," he says. "The crew strikes from this side. People enter from the other."

We dodge a palm tree and a giant moon. "I don't remember these," I say.

"They would have come in for the final dance," he says. "But it ended up being with you."

A line of dim floor lights leads us toward a set of enormous double doors.

"This is where the real fun is," Blitz says and keys in another code.

The lock pops and he pulls on the handle. One

side opens and another red light automatically switches on. He turns to me. "This will be a lark."

His expression is pure mischief. He leads me into the room.

Even bathed in red, it's astonishing. It's a storage room, big as a gymnasium, for all the props ever used on *Dance Blitz*.

I let go of his hand. "Oh! There's the boat from season one!" I turn around. "And the tiki hut from that Polynesian number! I loved that one!"

Blitz laughs. "That was a fun one."

I rush from one set piece to the next. There's the shell of a sports car, a motorcycle, two staircases set in clouds, and a partial interior of a malt shop. I sit on a stool and spin around. "Shake, please!" I say.

Blitz runs forward and leaps onto the counter like he did on the show, sliding along its surface to land in front of me. Then he grimaces. "That's a lot harder to do in jeans," he says.

I burst into giggles. "It still looked good!"

Another staircase sparkles red in the light. "I remember this!" I say and jump from the stool, running up the glittery steps. "Be a star where you are, be a star!" I sing out loud.

"Hey, you're not half bad!" he says. He jumps from the malt shop counter and follows me up the steps. He kisses my cheek, then turns and slides down the rail to the floor.

I gasp, then remember that he did it on the show. "No mat at the bottom or anything?" I ask.

"Nope," he says. "I perform all my own stunts."

He holds his hands up to me. I descend a few of the steps, then leap over the last few. He catches me neatly and slides me down his body. "It's way more fun on these props with you," he says.

"You just had to audition a lot of dancers before you got to me," I say against his cheek. He smells divine, like pine woods and diner food and leather.

"I knew you would love seeing all this," he says.

"So sad to think it will all go away."

"Other shows will use it. I think half these things came from previous dance productions."

I turn around, and then freeze. Blitz feels me go still. "What is it?" he asks.

In the corner, almost hidden by a volcano, is the red satin bed.

I walk toward it. It's still made up, as if somebody rolled it over and forgot about it. I smack my hand against the bedding, expecting an explosion of dust, but it's fine.

"Yeah, that," Blitz says. He runs a hand nervously through his hair. "They fixed it up again for the finale, in case I picked Giselle, but it just got shoved in the corner when we decided to go with the tropical theme."

I sit on it. It's an actual mattress, and it gives a

little. "This was one of the first *Dance Blitz* numbers I ever saw," I tell him.

"Really, that one? It definitely pushed the ratings into the stratosphere, starting off season two with a scandal and censored episode."

"I saw the audience photos. She got naked!"

Blitz lets out a rush of air. "She did. I don't know what she thought she was doing. They didn't let her back on the show after that."

"Did you want her back?"

He shakes his head. "No, she wasn't professional. And they were already planning on a live finale, and you can't let somebody like that be a part of it, even if there is a delay in the broadcast."

"Really, there's a delay?"

"Oh, yeah. The station can get shut down if something really bad goes on the air. FCC rules. There are engineers whose sole job is to bleep out anything not allowed, cuss words, or certain types of promotion. And nudity, of course."

"You seemed really...attracted to her in the shots," I say.

"I couldn't believe she had done it," Blitz says. "What you were seeing was utter disbelief."

My hands run along the silky bedspread. "I super jealous of that girl when I saw it."

Blitz lies down on his side, his head propped on

his hands. "At what point did you go looking up this gem?"

"After the first class with the wheelchair ballerinas. The second day I knew you."

"Ah. So you were stalking me already?"

I punch him lightly on the chest. "No!" Then, "Okay, maybe."

He grabs me around the waist and pulls me down on the bed. In a flash, I'm trapped beneath him, his knees on either side of my hips and his face looming over mine in the low light.

"Well, guess what?" he says.

"What?"

"I never saw her again, and this bed was never used."

I laugh. "Poor forgotten bed."

He reaches between us and unsnaps the top of my jeans. "Oh, no, not forgotten at all."

My eyes go wide and I glance around. "Here?"

He jerks the zipper down. "Oh, yes. Right here."

His mouth captures mine. I'm feeling a touch of panic. I mean, it's a big space! And people will be arriving for the contract meeting! Directors. Producers. Hannah. Uggh. Hannah. And Bennett!

But then his hand slips into the open jeans and I forget all that. His mouth is hot on me, still tasting of pie, and I groan as he revisits all the knowledge he has of my body, his fingers deep inside me.

I gasp against his mouth. My hips rise to meet him. His thumb works my little nub, and my body can't help but respond.

"I love this," he whispers against me. "And I love you."

He lifts his body and slides his hand out of me. Air hits my belly as he jerks my jeans down. "More naked or less?" he asks.

I glance around, my courage returning. The last girl on this bed bared herself in front of a studio audience.

"All the way," I tell him.

I don't have to say it twice. My jeans and panties are gone, my shoes flying. The red light disappears as the sweater flies over my face.

Jerry forgot to pack a bra, so that's it. I'm as naked as that girl.

"Lie back on the bed," Blitz says.

His face is intense as he looks at me. I obey, shifting back until I'm in the center, then I lie down.

"Oh, this is gonna make me lose it way faster than I want to," Blitz says. "Spread those thighs for me."

I brace myself up on my elbows and do as he asks, my legs sliding luxuriously over the cool silk bedspread until my ankles reach either side.

He lets out a long exhale and pulls his sweater over his head. He kicks off his shoes and unfastens his jeans. "I don't know what I want to do first," he says.

"Make it up as you go along," I say. He's outrageously hard, coming at me like a jungle cat, low and stealthy.

He crawls over my body, and I'm reminded of the dance he did with the girl, before she got naked. I hook a knee around his waist and slide around him. Now I'm straddling his back.

"Love it," he growls, and he gets it. We're dancing the way we sometimes do, naked, no music, all intensity and sex.

He kneels, partially sitting now, and reaches up to grasp my arms. With a sharp pull, he sends me falling toward the satin.

He leans down and licks my belly, his hair tickling my skin. Then he moves down, slipping his tongue between my thighs.

My back arches, and my body is seized by him. Everything is a swirl, the red lights, the satin, now rumpled in disarray. His mouth, his fingers, and I'm lost, spiraling up, my muscles tensing. He sucks hard and I just let go, over the top, my voice lost in the huge room, saying his name, Benjamin, Blitz, my love.

He brings me down carefully and moves his mouth to my belly, kissing my skin. He lets my breathing slow, inching forward until his erection presses against me.

"I'm going to take you so damn hard," he says, his voice gravelly and low.

Then we hear it.

The pop of the door.

"And this is where many of the props are kept," says a loud female voice.

"Shit," Blitz says. He yanks the satin bedspread off the mattress and scoops me up.

I can't even say anything in my panic. He dashes to the back side of the volcano and shoves his knee against a latch.

A back section pops open.

"Will we reuse any of these?" another female voice asks.

We duck inside the tall cavity of the volcano. Blitz turns and closes the door. It's pitch black in here.

"Who is that?" I whisper.

"Taya, one of the producers," Blitz says. "I don't recognize the other."

Blitz spreads the bedding on the cold floor and pulls me against him. "They might turn on all the overheads."

And sure enough, white light suddenly appears above us through a hole in the top of the volcano. It's still dim inside the prop, but I can see the shadowy figure of Blitz.

Naked Blitz.

Naked me.

In a volcano.

"It's fine," Blitz says. "They aren't going to come in here."

"But our clothes are out there."

He lets out a quiet laugh. "True. Maybe they won't notice."

God, the things I end up doing with Blitz Craven.

He runs his hands along my back and shoulders, massaging my anxiety away. We hear the muffled sounds of the women talking, but from inside the prop, we can't make out the words.

I can feel Blitz behind me, still hard as a rock. After a minute or two of waiting, his hands stray from my back to my belly, and up to my breasts. "God, you are one hot thing," he says into my hair. "Please don't ask me to stop."

I couldn't if I wanted to. His hand reaches around for me, and I fall forward, propped on my hands. My fingers clutch the satin as he works me again.

"Can't resist this," he says, his voice strangled. He bumps against me from behind, then he slips inside and I gasp, my hair falling forward, my body on fire.

He works me carefully, his fingers tight around front, his body giving me long easy strokes.

I'm going to lose it again, I can tell. The air is warm and my breasts are tingling. Blitz is trying to stay silent, and so am I. But he picks up speed and

I'm with him, pushing back, leaning down, wanting it hard and fast, and just like that I'm gone again, biting my own forearm, trying to be quiet.

Blitz's face is buried against my neck, his own groans muffled. We breathe in tandem, still locked together, as the voices outside get a little louder. Now we can actually hear words.

"Some of these pieces are almost iconic for the show, like this volcano," one says.

"Agreed. We'll definitely hang on to this."

Then silence, and the voices are muffled again.

Blitz pulls away from me. We sit together on the satin.

"How long do you think we'll have to sit here?" I ask.

Blitz flicks his watch face. The circle lights up in the dark. "Five minutes until the meeting," he says. "I'm guessing they're probably on their way out."

He's right, because a few seconds later, the white light goes out. It's pitch black inside the volcano again.

I sense Blitz moving, then I hear a click, and I spot a rectangle of red light where he's opened the back of the prop. I scramble for it, dragging the bedspread with me.

Blitz waits outside, strong and magnificent standing in the surreal glow. I almost want to take a picture.

"Are our clothes still there?" I ask.

"I can see your white sweater glowing," he says. "I think we're good."

We swiftly gather our things and pull them on. "I guess they were scattered enough that they didn't figure it out," I say.

"If they did, they let it go," Blitz says. "We'll see when we walk in the meeting."

God, the meeting. I try to manage my hair. It's all over the place, hair-sprayed to hell. As I step into my flats, I run my fingers through it and rapidly tame it into a fat bushy braid. I don't have a tie, so I just hold the end, looking around.

Blitz tosses the bedspread roughly on the mattress and we weave back through the props. I spot an arch of fake flowers and bows and walk up to it, jerking one of the loose pieces until several inches of ribbon comes free. I tie it around the bottom of the braid.

I guess I'm about as good as it gets to go into this meeting.

Chapter Six

I decide to be late. After Blitz shows me the door to the boardroom, I move on to a bathroom to fix myself up. I simply cannot walk in there with crazy hair and smelling like sex.

In the mirror, I untie the braid and create an updo that tucks in on itself. With a little water to turn the hairspray into glue, it holds.

When I'm clean enough and smell like soap instead of Blitz, I head back out, anxious to find out what will happen to the show.

I can hear strident voices before I get to the door.

"Blitz, don't throw away everything you've done over this!" That one is Hannah, sounding as perturbed as she did in the limo.

"Stop trying to force my hand!" Blitz shoots back.

I pause outside the closed door. For a second

people talk in lower tones, so I can't hear anything else. Then a voice I know well. Giselle, the red-haired finalist. "You played dirty for two seasons! Now we're going to!"

What is she doing here?

I shove hard on the handle. The door flies open so fast it smashes into the wall on the inside.

A dozen well-dressed, perfect people all turn to look at me. I see the three finalists first, still in their getups from the hostile takeover they attempted at the DVD shop this morning. And Blitz's manager Hannah, of course.

Then Blitz, red faced and as angry as I've ever seen him.

Then our friend Bennett, looking subdued.

The rest I don't know, all wealthy looking, some in suits, others in expensive casual wear. I spot two women that I figure were the ones who were in the prop room earlier.

"Look who decided to show up," Giselle says. "The little bitch who thinks she can ruin all of us."

My face flushes hot. Blitz gets up and comes over to me. "This is out of hand," he says. "And I'm not going to submit Livia to it." He takes my arm as if we're going to leave.

"Don't walk away or we'll sue you into your next lifetime," one of the men says coldly. "You have obligations to your financial backers, the network, and the staff."

Blitz pauses. I squeeze his hand, trying to pull myself together. "It's all right, Blitz. Let's hear them out," I say.

Giselle laughs. "Oh, that's rich. As if you are in charge."

One of the women says quietly, "Giselle, don't talk yourself out of the picture. These are negotiations, not ultimatums or blackmail." She flashes a stern look at the man who threatened to sue.

Bennett stands up. "So glad to see you again, Livia. It's always a pleasure. Please, take my seat."

I notice that there isn't a chair for me.

"We'll stand over here," Blitz says. "Because I want to make it clear that I'm prepared to walk."

"You're always so dramatic," Hannah says. "We're not proposing anything that preposterous."

Bennett sits back down. "Let's sort this out now that Livia is here. It concerns her."

Blitz puts his arm around me and holds me tightly by the waist. We stay by the door.

"What's on the table?" I ask, hoping I sound faintly businesslike.

The threatening man speaks up. "Bennett proposed a new format for the show focused on you and Blitz, not unlike the three episodes planned for the contest winner. Meet the parents, wedding plans, and so on."

My belly quavers. "I don't think my parents would agree," I say, glancing up at Blitz.

I can't involve them in any way. They aren't even speaking to me, but I don't want to tell these people that.

"They're not even engaged," Giselle spits out. "And happiness and bliss was never a selling point for the show. It's the competition."

"So you can whore yourself out," Blitz snaps.

I squeeze his hand again. I'm starting to see why he nearly lost his show over a Tweet about her. She really gets to him. I've never seen him like this.

"If I may," Bennett interjects. "After the finale, everyone expects Blitz to be with Livia. She has her own fan base, and a dozen Twitter handles have already appeared for her. I say we get her on board, build a show around the two of them, and ride out the contract."

A friendly-looking older man sitting next to the finalist Mariah reaches his hand out to the center of the table to get their attention. "I believe," he says, "that some form of compensation should be offered to the finalists for loss of income and publicity associated with the unscripted ending of the show."

Bennett speaks again, his face calm below his perfectly trimmed hair. His suit is flawless. He seems totally in control. It's obvious he manages situations like this every day.

"It isn't clear who the winner would have been. I'm aware we planned a dance around Mariah, but in all honesty, there were sets prepared for Giselle and Christy too. Blitz had the final say, and we agreed at this very table that he could make a last-minute choice based on the live events of the evening. So all contestants had an equal chance of losing, and the publicity they received after this unscripted finale was greater than it would have been if they had simply lost."

The lawyer sits back. Mariah frowns.

"What we don't know," Hannah says, "is what the future of *Dance Blitz* should be. We have a very popular franchise here, and we need to proceed carefully."

One of the women speaks up again. "I am not on board with a bland show about a couple in love. I don't think Livia is a strong dancer, and she can't carry the numbers."

My face flames hot, even though I know it's true.

"If we keep the competition aspect, then what are they competing for?" Bennett asks.

"It has to be dramatic," the threatening man says, his face blustery red. "There's no point in driving it into the ground."

"Just let the girls have it," Blitz says. "They can do

a *Bachelorette* and look for a male partner. I don't care. Just leave us out of it. I'm only dancing with Livia, and that's final."

With that, he leads me out into the hall.

We walk a ways down before I work up the courage to ask him how he's doing.

"That was open season on me back there," he says. "They can figure out what they want with the show. They can sue me. I don't really care if I ever work in this town again anyway."

We pass through the exit and crunch across the asphalt. The studios are quiet, although there is some activity several buildings down. Blitz punches angrily at his phone. "Trying to get the driver," he says.

It's mid-afternoon and beautiful out, sunshine and white clouds. It doesn't match Blitz's mood, though, and I just walk alongside him, trying to be a calm to his storm.

I don't know what the producers can do to him, but Bennett is definitely on our side, and a couple of the others seem as though they could be reasoned with. Surely we will all find a way to work it out.

Chapter Seven

◈

We had planned to stay in LA through Monday, but when we arrive at the hotel, Blitz gets on the phone with his travel agent and manages to book a flight for that evening.

"I'm sick of this city," he says as he tosses clothes into a suitcase. "Everybody is in it for fame and glory and nobody cares about anybody else."

I walk carefully around him, picking up my own things and painstakingly folding them in a perfect arrangement in my bag. I know he doesn't want to do the show anymore. I'm with him on that. But something about the finalists is really getting to him.

We've really only been together a couple of months. I'm not sure how to handle the rage version of Blitz. I wonder how much of him I haven't really seen.

"We have lots of time before we have to leave," I say. "Sit with me."

Blitz sighs and plops onto the bed next to me. "I'm sorry, Livia. I'm not doing so well with people forcing me to make long-term commitments I don't want."

"It's all right," I say. "That would get to anybody." I hold on to his hand. "What is so bad about doing the show?"

"It would be a huge fake," he says. "I would have to dance with those girls and pretend to be considering them. It was hard enough when I was half-interested in a few of them. It will be impossible now."

He presses his fingers against his eyes like he's tired. "I've made my own bed here. I know it."

"Giselle really made you mad," I say. "Big-time mad."

"She's the queen of manipulation," he says, his voice edgy. "I don't even know what she wants, just to be noticed, to make headlines, or what. It definitely isn't me. She was banging half the crew and trying to get in the pants of Tom."

"Tom?"

"The red-faced producer who threatened to sue."

"Oh, that lovely man."

"Right. He's trying to show he has balls by pushing me around. I'm sure she was probably blowing him in the bathroom before the meeting started."

"If all that is true, then they should be happy wrestling the show from you and leaving us out of it. Let the girls have their revenge auditions for male dancers of their own."

"I don't know if they'll go for it. The first season of *The Bachelorette* killed it, but after that, it just dropped like a stone."

"Well, then they should kill it with these girls, right? First season." I stand up, pacing the room. "It's perfect. Lots of drama. Dancing. Scandal. We don't need to have anything to do with it!"

Blitz leans forward, his elbows on his knees, his head in his hands. "There's a lot of money at stake here," he says. "A huge show. I don't know what they'll do."

I can see he's had enough. I kneel down in front of him and slip my fingers around the back of his neck. His muscles are in knots. "We'll get through this," I say. "It seems big, but it's not in your heart, you know? It's just business and career." I press my hand against his chest. "It's not going to affect what's in here."

He lifts his head and presses his palm on top of my hand. "You're right. How can we even worry about something as silly as a TV show when we have wheelchair ballerinas to train, and a little girl to watch grow up?"

"Their class is on Valentine's Day," I say. "I thought we could buy them all red sparkle sticks to dance with and take home."

He kisses my hand. "That sounds perfect." His eyes meet mine, dark and expressive. I can picture the camera close-ups from his show, how millions of women swooned over this very look. But it's real now. It's mine.

His mouth shifts into a mischievous grin. "Are you still going to love me when I'm sued into poverty and can't afford sparkle sticks for dancers?"

"Of course," I say. "I think when I showed up here in LA for that finale I had nothing but a backpack with a change of clothes."

"It's true," he says, pulling me to him so that our foreheads touch. "Not even a toothbrush."

"Also true," I say. "Just don't ask me to live with your parents."

He laughs. "Hell, no," he says. "I'll teach dance lessons to Weeza before I resort to that."

God, Weeza. She was a dancer from San Antonio who had called Blitz a sellout.

"We'll be fine," I say. "We better go or we'll miss that plane."

"Find your sunglasses," Blitz says. "We had a very public day and we're about to get on a commercial flight with the good citizens of California. We're bound to be spotted."

I pull a pair from my bag and slip them on. "I'm all over the incognito," I say.

Blitz pulls me onto his lap. "I could not get through all this without you," he says.

I kiss his ear. "You wouldn't be in all this mess without me," I say. "You'd just do the show."

"No way," he says. Then, "Well, okay, maybe. I guess I'd be pretending to plan a wedding with Mariah right now."

"I knew it!" I squeal. "She was the one!"

"You didn't think I would pick Giselle, did you?" he asks.

"I'm glad you didn't pick anybody."

"I'm supremely glad you chose me," he says.

There's a knock at the door.

"Here for our bags," Blitz says ruefully, looking over the unpacked disaster from all the activity that morning with wardrobe and makeup.

He sets me down and goes to the door. "Tell housekeeping to send some people up to pack all this and have it shipped," he tells the man outside. "We're traveling light."

Blitz turns to me and waves me over. I grab my purse and shift the sunglasses on my head. At the last minute, I grab a scarf from a box on the wardrobe rack.

"Good call," Blitz says, and rummages through a plastic bin. He produces a newsboy cap and sticks it jauntily on his head. "Very not me," he says.

"Adorable," I tell him.

We pass by the man, who nods at us, and head downstairs to find our driver and move on to the airport. I can't wait to put LA behind us.

When we get downstairs, though, it's a different car.

"Well, hell," Blitz says when he sees the dusky blue Jaguar. "I guess that answers one question."

I hang on to his arm as a man in a cowboy hat gets out and walks around to open the back door.

"I've seen this car before," I say, right as I remember where. It's in all the pictures on all the dates of Blitz and the contestants. It's *his* car.

"Come on, now, don't waste any more time," the man says in a deep Texas drawl. "You gotta flight to catch."

Blitz hesitates, then lets me loose so he can shake the man's hand. They thump each other heartily on the back.

I don't recognize him. But Blitz turns around and gestures to him. "It's probably about high time you met my best friend and bodyguard. Livia, this is Duke."

"Nice to finally see you in person," Duke says, extending a hand.

"You actually exist," I say. "I've heard about you."

"All bad, I'm sure," Duke says.

"What are you doing here?" Blitz asks.

Duke grins. "Hannah's stooges checked up on me, figuring I was selling your half-used bars of soap on the black market."

"Were you?"

"Hell, no, you ain't worth a plugged nickel now that you're practically hitched." He winks at me. "Anyway, they said I better resume my duties or I was fired. I came on down to see what's what with you."

"Holed up in the hometown," Blitz says. "Trying to get away from a pissed-off public."

"I saw you kissed a pig at a rodeo," Duke says with a laugh. Behind the blue Jaguar, a limo pulls up and honks. "Assholes," Duke says, then he calls out, "Your celebrity ain't any bigger than my celebrity!"

"It's all right," Blitz says. He leads me to the door and I duck inside.

As I slide across the seat, I remember what Blitz told me early on about all the cameras installed inside. He'd bought a new car to drive to Texas to avoid unauthorized footage of him.

I look around anxiously. I don't spot anything obvious.

Blitz closes his door. He also glances at the ceiling, floor, and doors.

"Would we know if we're being recorded?" I ask.

"Nope," Blitz says. "Although I know there was one here." He pushes a button on a rectangle of metal in the ceiling and a screen pops down. Loose wires spring out.

Duke gets in the car and slams his door. He glances back as he buckles up and says, "Oh, I scrubbed the car. No cameras."

"You just jerked them out?" Blitz asks, stuffing the wires back against the screen to close the lid.

"Pretty much," Duke says. "I didn't do your place, though. That's wired so hot you'll probably have to level it to get them all."

Blitz sits back. "I'll just sell it," he says. "I'll need the money anyhow."

Duke pulls away from the hotel. "That Giselle chick sue your ass into oblivion or what?"

"Nah, she dropped her suit for a new tactic. I quit the show."

Duke doesn't respond to that, merging into traffic.

Twilight is starting to fall, and streetlights pop on ahead.

"So what's your next step?" Duke asks. "Should I ride this wave until it crashes or find another line of work?"

"It's not settled yet," Blitz says. "They'll keep you on the payroll until I say."

Duke catches my eye in the rearview mirror. The

car isn't terribly big. "So what's your story, Livia? You grow up in San Antone?"

"I moved there four years ago," I say. "From Houston."

"That's one hell of a city," Duke says. "Couldn't pay me to live there. All the traffic of LA but none of the eye candy." We stop at a light and a girl in a bikini top and jeans saunters in front. He honks at her. She doesn't look.

"Not with me in the car, Duke," Blitz says. "I've got enough attention right now."

"Now that's the whole truth and nothing but the truth," Duke says. "You check out Twitter today?"

"Been avoiding it," Blitz says.

Duke messes with his phone, and when the light turns green, he tosses it back to us. "Check out what's trending."

The phone lands on the seat between us. Blitz ignores it, but I pick it up. "Did you post that picture of the girls in blue from the signing?" I ask him.

"No," he says. "I can do that." He pulls his own phone out of his pocket.

But as I look at all the Tweets about Blitz since the images of the finalists hit the media this morning, I hold out my arm. "I wouldn't say a word right now," I tell him.

"Why?"

I don't want to tell him. It's not as bad as the

#BurnBlitzBurn that trended when he was in trouble. But it's close.

There are pages and pages, as far as I can scroll, all saying the same thing.

#DanceBlitzRematch

Chapter Eight

When we land in Texas and turn our phones back on, Blitz's notifications go berserk. Everybody wants to talk to him about the Twitter trend, the possibility of letting me and the three finalists do a dance-off. All the entertainment shows, the big websites, several newspapers, and at least three network news reporters have inquired.

Blitz quits looking at them after we get off the plane, but I take his phone and continue to scroll through as we walk through the airport. Two girls notice him as we head toward the exit, but they are quiet and easily placated with a quick signature on their arms. I'm grateful there isn't a mob and a thousand questions about the rematch.

Ted picks us up, and I'm glad to see him. Duke was nice, but I'm not sure I trust him. Blitz is subdued, and nobody talks as we drive back to the hotel.

Blitz's bad mood doesn't lift even when we're inside our suite, the city lights of San Antonio twinkling outside the huge windows. I'm not sure what to do to help him.

He sits on the floor by the windows, looking out. I curl up next to him, my head on his shoulder.

"Want to talk about it?" I ask.

He's quiet for a while, then finally says, "I'm worried about what the show will do to you."

I sit up. "Me? Why are you worried about me?"

"Taya already talked about your dance skills. It's brutal out there, Livia. People are damn cruel. They'll pick apart your hair, your body, your dance, what you eat, what you say, where you come from. And they wonder why Hollywood is notorious for its addicts and suicides."

I lean my head on his shoulder again. I'm not sure what to say. I'd like to think that after years of feeling nothing but shame and self-misery, inflicted by my own father, I would hold up to any fire.

But maybe I'm not strong. Maybe years of solitude and guilt would only make me more vulnerable than most. My wounds might open easily, and I don't have a big support network to catch me. My family isn't speaking to me. I was homeschooled throughout high school, so I don't have a friend network. My best friend's family blocked my number so I can't reach her.

But I do have Bennett in my corner. And his wife Juliet. And Dreamcatcher Dance Academy. Danika. Betsy. Aurora. Suze.

"I'll just have to get better," I say. "Maybe double up. Dreamcatcher and Jenica's." My voice almost falters, just saying it out loud. Our one experience at Jenica's Dancery was intense and scared the crap out of me. But I'd do it. For Blitz.

Blitz slides his arm around me. "You amaze me every day, Livia. There is nothing you won't try."

"For us," I say. "I wouldn't do jack diddly for Hannah."

He laughs. "You might need your own manager in the end."

The room is quiet, although from across the room I can hear the new notification I set up on my phone for #DanceBlitzRematch. Every few seconds, there's another soft ping, another person agreeing that this is what they want to see. Another piece of evidence to the producers about the way the show should go.

~*´ ` *~

THE NEXT DAY WE TAKE BLITZ'S RED FERRARI OUT

to a dance shop in a quiet part of town to pick up red sparkle sticks for the wheelchair ballerinas.

It's Sunday, and the city is already preparing for spring, because Texas doesn't have much of a winter. Along the streets, *piñata* vendors hang their oversized Tweety Birds and princesses out on porches. Men push metal freezer carts full of ice cream and cups of frozen fruit.

I love these parts of San Antonio because I never saw them before Blitz. He knows all the *mercados*, big and small, the tiny *taquerias* with the best tamales, and where to find flamboyant tights you can't find in normal shops.

We generally don't have to worry about fan sight-ings or getting mobbed by crazy girls in these places. Everyone is friendly, and even if they recognize Blitz, nobody asks for more than a handshake and a smile.

In general, the car attracts more attention than we do. Several men line up to run their hands along the Ferrari's hood as we park on the street in front of a low-key dance store that doubles as a place to buy dresses and accessories for a girl's *quinceañera*.

Blitz gives the men a nod and leads me up the wood steps to the shop, which is a converted house nestled in the middle of a neighborhood.

Dresses with miles of ruffles hang over the porch. Inside the door are glass cases full of lacy accessories and guest books and pillows.

"I guess there isn't an equivalent of a *quinceañera* for boys?" I ask, fingering another dress that is an explosion of tulle and netting, like a wedding dress, only in pink.

"Fifteen-year-old boys do not want a fancy party," Blitz says, scanning the place. "It's bad enough having to go to the girls'. Dance stuff over here."

I linger on the dresses. Gabriella doesn't have any sort of Mexican heritage, but I picture her in one of the dresses anyway, her long black hair flowing down.

Then I realize in my image of her, she is standing up, and I shake it from my thoughts. I've never known exactly what happened during the car accident that killed her adopted father and injured her, but I know it was bad. I saw pictures of her in the hospital on Facebook. They were dark days, ones I could not see her through.

"Can I help you?" a woman asks. She is tall and elegant in a sheath dress, dressed very chic for a shopkeeper. She must do well with her *quinceañera* dresses, or else feels she must look a certain way to sell them.

Blitz speaks to her a moment in Spanish, and I turn to the racks of dance outfits. Most of them are for little girls, tutus and leotards in every bright color. Gwen, Gabriella's mother, must shop at a place like this, as all the stores I've ever been to seem to only have variations of pink, white, and black.

The woman leads Blitz to another room and I drift slowly that direction. Every place I look, I see more beautiful objects. I want to take them all in. I feel exceptionally lucky in that moment. I could buy any of these things if I wanted. Blitz has been very generous. But I have no income of my own. I do nothing at all to help.

We live in a hotel, eating room service or the specific foods sent by Blitz's trainer to stay in dance shape. I don't clean or do laundry or even pick up around the suite. That is all handled by the staff.

I do teach the wheelchair ballerina class, but that is a volunteer position. I'm not qualified for anything.

I never even applied for college, because I left the SAT site without completing all the tests I signed up for, which disqualifies your results. At least that's what the website says. But even if they sent me results, my father signed me up and therefore had the scores sent to him. I'll never see them.

Who am I without Blitz? What would I do if something happened to him? To us?

My throat tightens.

I really should figure out something of my own.

Blitz reappears from the side room holding up a clear stick filled with glitter and stars. On one end is a heart, on the other, a trail of red ribbons.

"Is it perfect or what?" he asks.

My chest swells just looking at him, one of the

most famous people in this town, picking out toys for young girls. What does he want? Could it really be to live a quiet life with only me? No show, no fame, no publicity?

"It is," I manage to say. "Do they have enough of them?"

"She's checking," he says. He twirls the stick through his fingers and tosses it in the air. But he doesn't consider the low ceiling and smacks it, showering popcorn paint bits into his hair.

"Oops." He steps quickly to the side to catch the errant stick before it hits the hardwood floor.

I laugh and step forward, brushing the ceiling bits out of his hair. "At least we know it's a tough prop."

"True. They'll probably hit the floor more often than not." He smacks the stick against his hand and checks the toughness of the attached heart.

The woman takes a long time. We wander around. No one else is inside. I peek out the door and see several more men gathered around Blitz's car. This would unnerve me, as I generally don't like to attract attention, but Blitz is always laid back about it. I guess you don't buy a car like that without expecting people to look at it.

"I'm going to go find her," Blitz says.

I look down the street a bit and notice a gathering of young women with their phones. They are all talking excitedly and showing each other their screens.

I never had a big group of friends like that, although in middle school, when I still got to go to public school, two or three of us hung out together. My family couldn't afford a cell phone for me, but my friend Laura had one. She was always texting a boy named Erik, who was obviously sexy because his name had a "k."

The thought makes me smile.

Another car pulls up to the shop. And another. The girls on their phones look over at the door near where I'm standing.

Why would so many people be arriving here at the same time?

The new girls jump out of their car and wave their arms excitedly toward the shop. One of them has on a Blitz shirt.

Oh, no.

I jerk my own phone out of my pocket. I hurry to Twitter and check the #BlitzSighting hashtag.

It's insane. Everyone is sharing and retweeting the address of the dance store.

We've been found.

I hurry through the shop. Blitz is not in the next room. There's a door in the back wall. I don't really want to go through it. What if the back part of this house is where they live?

I pause to knock. "Blitz?" I ask and wait. No answer. Was there another way back? I glance around.

Then I realize — phone. I text him a quick note. *We've been sighted. Mob descending.*

Within seconds, a door I didn't notice, tucked in a corner behind a rack, pops open.

Blitz storms out empty-handed and pulls on my arm. "The owner did it," he says. "I caught her sending out a picture."

He pulls me to the front door.

As soon as we step out, dozens of cell phones lift into the air.

"Great, just great," Blitz says. He plasters on a smile and waves.

We try to head straight for the car, but the crowd surges forward.

"This is nuts," I say as we push through. "How did so many get here so quick?"

"She sent out a Tweet before we even got on the porch," he says, opening my door, waving at everybody, but firmly keeping them back.

The first girl shouts, "Blitz, I love you!" and then the noise just erupts. They wave paper, pens, notebooks, phones. Blitz manages to shut my door, but he's completely trapped trying to get around to his side.

He signs a few things, still trying to smile, and attempts to walk forward.

But the girls are aggressive. One of them starts shouting, "Rematch, rematch!" and the whole group takes up the chant. From my spot inside the car, I can see at least five live Facebook feeds are broadcasting them.

I'm about to open my door and scream at the lot of them when a couple of the men who had been looking at the Ferrari take charge and start pushing them back.

Blitz manages to go around the front of the car and get to the opposite door.

Then he's in.

"I guess we're not going anywhere else public for a while," Blitz says as he starts the car. When the engine rumbles, the crowd steps back.

"This wasn't happening before," I say. "We've been going to restaurants and shopping for clothes, and we haven't had more than a few passersby stop and chat or ask for a picture."

"It's got to be the finalists," Blitz says, dropping the car into gear. A couple girls try to get in front of us, but the men pull them back so he can get a clear path out onto the street.

"What are they up to?"

"They must have social media people scouring for mentions and blowing them up."

I open my phone again. I check for #BurnBlitz-Burn but there isn't much there. The #BlitzSighting is huge right now, but I go back and back through time until I spot older mentions of his whereabouts to see if I can connect any dots.

Then I see it. A Twitter profile called "DanceBlitzRematch" has been promoting Tweets that show our current location. It has maps and even offers prizes, free DVDs and T-shirts, to people who post live updates if they see him and start the "rematch" chant. It is only two days old and already has half a million followers.

I lean my head back against the headrest.

"I'm guessing you found the source," he says.

"Who does your social media?" I ask.

"There's several of them," Blitz says, eyes on the road as he carefully eases away from the crowd.

"They've got a whole account set up to promote the rematch," I tell him. "They are offering incentives to fans to start the chants anywhere they can spot us."

Blitz slams his hand on the steering wheel. "They just won't let up, will they?"

"Let's fight fire with fire," I say. "Have your people put up fake location spottings to decoy them away from us."

Blitz laughs. "Love it. I bet I can get Duke to drive my old car around LA and get the sightings even more credibility."

"If they think we're in LA, then we can discredit

the ones that are real," I say.

"I'll get them on it," Blitz says. "Because I really don't want crazy people showing up at Dreamcatcher."

"Exactly," I say, my heart hammering. "And we can't live like this."

"I've been living this way for two years," Blitz says. "But I do think it's time I got the gray rental back. This car is just too obvious."

"I know exactly who to have drive it around town," I tell him, then get a case of the giggles so bad that when we stop at a red light, Blitz has to thump me on the back so I can catch air.

He's laughing too. "What is your evil mind cooking up now?"

"We'll give this car to the bodyguard, Ted. He'll handle the crowds."

Blitz nods. "I like it. And that boy could use a real set of wheels."

We get on the highway for a while, making sure none of the zealous girls are trying to follow us. Our hotel is pretty secure, used to celebrities and politicians, but there is no point in making it easy to find us.

We'll up our game to keep our privacy, but one thing is pretty obvious now.

We're going to have to deal with the three finalists.

Chapter Nine

W e succeed at getting to Dreamcatcher
Tuesday morning without anyone following.
Suze looks up from the front desk with a grim smile.
"Y'all are trending again on Twitter," she says. "Every-
body wants a rematch."

Danika catches us in the hall. "I'm keeping the
security," she says. "The mob at the dance shop made
the news and I can't have that here."

Blitz and I glance at each other. We already
caused enough trouble with my ex Denham showing
up and requiring Danika to get a restraining order.
His getting arrested out front cost the academy quite
a few dancers.

"If we need to take a break, we will," Blitz says.

I can't imagine not getting to see Gabriella, but

Danika just waves her hand. "We'll work around it. Just do your part not to be followed. I'll be on top of any mothers who think it will be fun to say you are here."

We head back to the studios, where Janel has already begun to warm up the wheelchair ballerinas.

The girls love their sparkle sticks, ones we sent a courier to retrieve from a different shop, and we dance with them for the allotted hour. But what should have been an escape feels hollow and strained. The mothers send us sympathetic glances. More than one keeps checking the hall as if they expect a crowd to surge in at any moment.

"We can't keep this up," I say to Blitz as we get in the car after class. "We don't have the setup to handle this level of privacy invasion."

"Nobody does," Blitz says. "But one good thing about the public is its short attention span. I really think this will die down in a few days."

I hope he's right. As we drive a circuitous route back to the hotel, I wonder what we're even going to do for Valentine's Day. I have a gift for Blitz, not much since I don't really have money of my own right now, but I'm hoping we get to celebrate it somehow.

When we get back to our suite, I ask him, "Are we staying in tonight?"

He falls back on the sofa. "I have reservations at

an amazing place, but I'm not sure they are going to be thrilled about dealing with our level of crazy at the moment."

"Do they have celebrities often?" I ask.

"Probably, but San Antonio just isn't that kind of town. It's not like New York or LA or even DC, where lots of places have protocol in place. Here they rely on being expensive and having valet parking to keep the public at bay."

"You just want to stay here?" I stand at the end of the white sofa, looking down at him. I'm filled with uncertainty.

"Come here," he says, waving his arms at me.

He's taking up the whole sofa, so I lie on top of him and tuck my head against his shoulder.

"I'm happy doing whatever," I say.

"Me too," he says, kissing my hair. "But I really don't like three pain-in-the-ass women controlling our lives."

"Technically, it's their Twitter feed," I say.

He goes still. "What did you say that Twitter account was called?"

"DanceBlitzRematch," I say.

"Huh. Hold on." He shifts us a little to pull his phone out of his pocket and taps a contact.

I listen to his heartbeat as it rings. Then someone picks up.

"Hey, it's Blitz Craven. Is Larry around?"

He pauses. Larry is his lawyer.

"No, no, don't bother him. Just tell him that we have a trademark violation on Twitter. The account is DanceBlitzRematch. I'd like it down as fast as he can make that happen. Thanks."

He kills the call. "That will take care of that."

"Assuming it's not one of the producers who can lay claim to the trademark," I say. "There was that one guy."

Blitz lifts my chin so he can meet my eyes. "How did I get such a smart girl to look at me twice?" he asks.

I shrug. "I always assume the worst."

"I say we go out anyway. I'll have someone go in ahead and make sure the way is clear."

"If the staff doesn't turn you in themselves."

"You really do assume the worst," he says, kissing my hair again.

"It's a gift."

He sits up and shifts me next to him. "I have something that will cheer you up," he says.

He heads over to the bar and opens a cabinet where one of the safes is hidden. When he turns back, he's holding a small flat box in shiny red wrapping paper.

"For my Valentine," he says. "If you don't like it, we can get something else."

I take the box. It's light. Too small for a necklace. Too flat for a ring. I already have a cell phone, and besides, it jingles a little when I shake it. A bracelet, maybe?

I pull the ribbon loose and tear away the colored paper. I've never had a Valentine, actually. I knew boys in middle school, but I never had one as a boyfriend. High school was spent at home. Dad usually brought a box of chocolates home for the family to share.

The paper falls away and I lift the lid.

Inside is a set of car keys.

"Blitz?" I ask.

"All yours," he says. "I really hope you like it."

My heart hammers. A car?

"Can I see it?"

"It's already waiting downstairs."

I snatch up my sunglasses and scarf. "Let's go!"

We race to the elevator. We're halfway down when I realize something important.

"I can't drive it!" I exclaim. "I still don't even have my permit!"

"Nobody's going to care," Blitz says. "You're getting good enough."

"I should have gone to the DMV before all this stuff happened," I say. "Now they'll find us for sure if I show up someplace that public."

We step onto the elevator and Blitz wraps his

arms around me. "It'll die down. Don't worry. And I'll see if we can't arrange for you to go in before they open. Surely someone can be bribed."

"It's the DMV," I say. "They live to laugh at people who think they can get special favors."

"I hear I'm pretty charming." Blitz flashes that megawatt smile that has gotten him two million Twitter followers. It works. If anybody could sweet-talk the DMV, it's him.

The doors slide open for the lobby. We walk cautiously to the front doors.

"The concierge is aware of the situation," Blitz says. "He knows to alert us if anyone figures out we're here."

But everything is normal, other than six pretty cars sitting outside.

"Which one is mine?" I ask, practically bouncing with excitement.

"Which one do you think?" Blitz asks. His smile is enormous.

I look around. "I'm guessing not the green SUV with an inch of mud on the tires."

"Good observation," he says.

"And I don't think the black Mercedes is what you'd pick for me."

"Nope."

"I'm guessing the white Volkswagen convertible!"

"We have a winner!" Blitz says.

I rush over to the car. "I love it!" I say.

"Let's go for a spin, then," Blitz says.

I glance around. "I've never driven on an actual street, remember?" I say.

"It's easy," Blitz says. "And you were doing great in the parking lot last time."

I walk around to the driver's side. A uniformed man opens my door.

The new car smell wafts out. It's all leather and something I can't define.

I sit down as Blitz settles in on the passenger side. "I've never smelled a new car before. Yours always smelled like French fries."

"Guilty as charged," Blitz says. "But this one only has the mileage the sales guy drove it to get here."

I glance at the dash. Eleven miles. Wow.

The bellman closes the door. I hold the keys but realize the key part isn't showing to put in the ignition. "How do you work this thing?"

"It's actually keyless," Blitz says. "Just put your foot on the brake and push this button."

I feel around for the gas and brake pedals and press the brake. When I push the big round button, the car's quiet engine purrs lightly.

"It's so cute!" I say.

"Ready to put it in drive?" he asks.

I look around me. There's still several cars I have

to navigate around. "Can I wait until they are all gone?" I ask.

"Sure," he says. "You probably need to adjust your mirrors anyway."

We fiddle around with the knobs and levers and get the seat the way I want it. By then, only the Mercedes is still in the circle drive, and it's behind us.

"Okay," I say. "Here goes." I slide the gear shift into drive and release the brake. We glide forward.

My brain tries to panic but I calm it down and slowly putter away from the front doors of the hotel.

"I'd go left," Blitz says. "You don't want to get mixed up in the traffic beneath the freeway."

I nod, concentrating, and turn on the signal.

This back street is quiet, and other than making sure I don't get too close to cars parked along the curb, the drive is easy.

"You're doing it!" Blitz says. He makes a big show of leaning his seat back and tucking his hands behind his head, as if he's going to take a nap.

"So what happens if I get pulled over?" I ask.

"We call Larry back," Blitz says.

Right, lawyers can handle anything.

We cruise around the neighborhood. I pass the academy, and the playground where I used to take my brother, and even my old house. Mom's minivan is in the carport, but I don't see any sign of them.

When Blitz notices where we are, he sits up. "You want to stop by? Your dad is probably at work."

I shake my head. "Not today. I'm having a good day. I don't want to wreck it."

"Or the car," Blitz says with a laugh.

I focus on the road. "Distract me and I *will* wreck it," I say.

"I'll be good," he says.

I meander the streets, passing my old church and the movie theater where I had an early date with Blitz. I feel so free, able to go anywhere I want, do anything. I have to get my license!

The concentration gets tiring after a while, so I head back to the hotel. I pull into the circle easily.

The valet opens the door and I have to keep myself from hugging him, instead content to jump up and down. I have a car!

Blitz comes around to take my hand, laughing at my exuberance. "This might be the best reaction to a gift ever!" he says.

Suddenly my Valentine present for him seems woefully inadequate. "Where are we going tonight?" I ask.

"Milan's," he says.

"We went there with that executive once, right?" I ask.

"Yes, the one who wanted to do Blitz dance wear."

We cross the lobby into the hotel. It's busier now.

Lots of couples are wandering around holding hands. They seem to be staying the night for the holiday.

We head up the elevator. I think about my gift for him and how I might spice it up. By the time we get to the top, I have an idea.

Chapter Ten

❧

When we get upstairs, Blitz changes for the workout room. I tell him I'm skipping for now and wait for him to leave before heading to my closet to find my gift for him.

Buried below my flannel pajamas, which never see any wear at all, is one long beautiful length of aerial silk for performing in the air.

I've watched all of *Dance Blitz*, plus most of Blitz's early works, and he has never done aerial silk dancing. But I watched as his eyes lit on the girl who was practicing at Jenica's Dancery the one time we went, and I knew I wanted to try it.

I learned all I could about the type of fabric that was used, how much to buy, and the width and length. I also began doing extra arm workouts, so

DEANNA ROY

when it was time to start learning, I would have the strength.

The strong red fabric came from a discount shop where I got it for a steal, less than Blitz would pay for lunch. I hemmed the ends and kept it hidden for today.

Watching YouTube videos had gotten me a few basics. I figured out that the very corner of the bed, where the top section meets the wall, is securely braced. It holds my weight, although probably not Blitz's. I use it to practice.

I have just enough moves to start. Blitz keeps talking about finding something that is only ours, and I think this could be it.

But after the car, I feel the need to up my Valentine game even more. It isn't enough to just dance with the silks. I want it to *be* us, something unique, something that involves memories that will carry us through performances and give us that extra magic.

And today will be the first one.

I draw in a deep breath. I'm really not an exhibitionist. I only wear makeup when someone comes to fix me up for an event. And while I have some rather lovely undergarments that we got when Blitz initially set up my wardrobe, we are really more of a workout pants and T-shirt couple.

But not today. I have to be different. Bold.

I rummage through the drawers to see what I

have that will go with the red fabric. There's definitely a red bra and matching panties, but they are sort of ordinary. I keep digging and find a white thong. Okay, this might do.

My heart hammers as I search. There are sheer things, lacy things, dainty things. But nothing as sexy as what I want to go for.

I'm going to have to improvise.

I find a pretty white bra.

"Sorry," I say to it as I walk through to the bathroom and find a pair of tiny sharp scissors. My face flames a little even though I'm alone as I alter the bra. With a couple easy snips, I've cut out the centers of the cups, heart-shaped bits of fabric fluttering to the floor.

Holy hell, am I really going to do this?

Then I pick up the thong and think — hmm. There isn't much to it, but how much more fun if it matched?

A few snips later and three hearts are cut out. A tiny one near the top, a medium one, then a larger one that means the underwear doesn't have to come off, even when it's time.

I heat up a little just looking at it. *Whoa*. I scoop up the five white hearts and take them to the bedroom, scattering them on the bed.

Then I take the red fabric and toss it over the reinforced corner of the bed, double-checking one more time that the giant screws holding it to the wall are tight and unmoving.

Now to wait.

Blitz has a definite ritual when he comes back from workouts. He'll go straight to the bar and drink more water. Then he'll go from the living area to the bathroom by the outside door. If I close the door between the bedroom and the bathroom, he won't look this way.

I check the clock. Still twenty minutes.

I slip out of my clothes and put on the white panties and underwear. My cheeks get hot as I see where all the open hearts land. Then I throw on a pair of loose sweats and move to the bathroom.

I braid my hair up and away. I pull out mascara and lipstick and eyeliner from the kit left by the wardrobe crew. I make myself up carefully but simply, layering on color and lines. When I'm done, I look different, older, more exotic. He will like it. He loves his innocent Livia, but he will totally lose it over my proof that I can be someone else, act a part.

I remember what that woman Taya said at the contract meeting, that I wasn't up for doing a show with Blitz. We have no intention of meeting any of their demands, but I feel some satisfaction in knowing that I could. I can be someone else, grab the attention of not only the sweet blue-dressed Livias outside the DVD signing, but also others. Viewers who expect a little dazzle.

I am perfectly happy letting no one see it but Blitz.

I head back into the living room, carefully closing all the doors to the bedroom.

Then I sit at the corner desk, my back to the door, and read through the Twitter feed until Blitz returns.

As always, he chugs a bottle of water from the bar fridge and heads to the bathroom. "Be out in a flash," he calls over to me.

I give him a "mm-hmm" and don't look his way.

He takes lightning-fast showers, so as soon as I hear the water hit the tile, I jump up, close the door from the bathroom to the living room to drive his path into the bedroom, and cross back into the room.

Then I close the blinds most of the way, until only fine lines of light stripe the bed. I take off the sweats and leave the white underwear, which glow a little in the half-dark.

I take a deep breath. Dang, I'm nervous for someone doing something with a man I've lived with for months. I carefully pop open the door to the bathroom, letting in another shaft of light.

Then I head to the bed.

I push the regular sheer fabric that surrounds it

up and away. I move to my red silks and wrap the ends around my ankles, then twist my wrists through.

And I wait, listening.

The water slows, then stops. The glass door squeaks open. His footsteps pad on the floor. The suite is so quiet that I can hear his towel rubbing against his hair.

His clothes are all in here, so I know he'll walk in naked. It will be easy to see his reaction to me.

I slowly exhale a nervous breath. I'm glad I've practiced this position, or my arms and legs would already be tired.

"So, Livia?" Blitz calls. "How dressy do you want to get for Milan's?"

I don't answer, so he comes into the bedroom.

He halts when he sees the lines of light, eyes looking for me. He's about to hit the switch when his hand freezes.

He's spotted me, all right.

There isn't a lot of vertical space on a bed rail, even with a canopy like this one, to do a lot of fancy moves. But I have a few tricks. The first one is where I pull up on the silks and my legs spread into splits. Then, I take a quick dramatic flip down and back up.

"Holy shit," he says. "When did you learn to do that?"

He starts to approach, then pauses, as I slowly

shift into a different position, a front and back split with arms outstretched.

"That's beautiful." He steps closer. "You're beautiful."

I adjust my weight so that I face him again. I know the minute he sees the heart cutouts, because his body instantly reacts.

"Okay, that is just wow," he says.

I pull myself high and untwist my legs from the silks. Once my feet are safely on the mattress, I free my hands. "So you liked it?" I ask.

He takes me into his arms, my belly at his face since he's still standing on the floor while I'm up on the bed.

"Like it? This is like the hottest thing anyone has ever done."

"I remembered the girl doing it at Jenica's," I say.

"You went back there? I thought it scared the crap out of you."

"No, I learned from YouTube," I say. "But if we maybe wanted to learn some moves together, I would go."

He reaches around me to twist his hand through the fabric. "That could be fun. Can I get you to do it naked?"

My face heats up.

"I'll take that as a silent yes," he says. "But first, I must admire your outfit."

He lets go of the silks and runs a finger along the underside of my bra strap. "These are some perfectly placed Valentines." He makes it to the cup and his thumb grazes across the opening, making my nipple pucker.

I suck in a breath. "My hearts are all yours," I say.

"And there are so many of them." His hand slides down my ribs to the tiny ribbon that holds the thong in place. He bends down to plant a kiss on the tiny heart at the top.

"One," he says, then goes lower to the next heart. "Two."

And down.

"Mmm, three." His hand parts my thighs and his mouth is against my skin through the opening of the heart. His tongue finds its way to the bud as his hand works its way back up to the bra.

I steady myself with my hands on his shoulders as he spreads me wider, then he pulls away. "Let's see that again." He grasps one of the silks and slides it around my ankle.

I know what he wants. I step back and wrap my other leg around the second length of the silk. Then I twist my arms through and lift back into the splits.

"Oh, yes," he says. "That's what I was going for."

He doesn't force me to hold the position on my own, but braces my thighs with his hands as he goes back to where he was, his mouth flirting with my body.

I'm open so wide, so much more with the pressure of the silks and the support of his hands. I feel both bold and vulnerable, and the sensations as he works are fierce, sending lightning strikes through me.

His tongue delves in and he sucks on the nub, and I'm lost, barely holding on to the silks. He rocks me gently, and the intensity of this motion makes goose bumps break out across my skin.

I lose my grip and slip a few inches, and he catches me, unwinding the fabric from my ankles.

I'm on a knife's edge, barely holding back from crashing over and beyond. Blitz lets my legs down, but instead of freeing my arms, wraps the silks more tightly around them.

"Now you're really at my mercy," he says, his voice gravelly and low. He tugs at the thong, pulling it down.

My arms are high in the silks, captured, tied, my back against the pillowed leather that serves as the headboard to the bed.

Blitz kneels on the mattress and puts my knees over his shoulders. Then he's back on me, his mouth and tongue working my body, his hands pressing me hard against him.

I'm already so close that I build into a frenzy

almost instantly, my hands gripping the silks, my body rocking against him. I start to go, the climax just ready to ripple through me, when Blitz grabs my legs and flips me around.

Now I face the wall, my arms still high, and he's inside me, pressing me against the cushioned leather. Everything lets go, and I can't control the ferocity of the orgasm, my voice almost at a scream, my muscles tight and shaking.

Blitz pushes against me again and again, his own body hard and forceful. I pull myself up by the silks and slam back down, wanting him deeper, harder, as intense as I feel.

He groans against my hair and I feel it, the hot rush of him. His body shudders and his head falls against my shoulder.

We stay this way for a moment, unable to come down from the position or the explosive high. Then he reaches up and unwinds the fabric from my wrists. We tumble down to the bed together.

Blitz lies back, his breathing still ragged. "That was a totally wicked dance, and I will never look at a silk scarf the same way again."

I roll over to curl against him and smile to myself. That was exactly what I was hoping for.

Chapter Eleven

W e almost blow off Milan's, but looking out on the city after our bit of aerial silks experimentation, we decide to go out anyway.

"I should get a blond wig," I say. I head to the bathroom to let down my braids, which are fuzzy and wild after our tussle.

"The paparazzi are relentless," Blitz says, coming behind me to play with my wavy post-braid hair. "And I like you just the way you are."

I lean back against him. We're both in white robes. He lifts the sleeves to inspect my wrists.

"No burn marks? No pain?" he asks.

I shake my head. "Nope. I've practiced."

He leans against the sink. "You really want to go back to Jenica's to work on this?"

I shrug back at the mirror, trying to fix my

smudged lipstick. "We could look for someone else," I say.

"No, I'll call over there. Somebody was training that girl. And I'm not sure how many places do aerial work."

He heads to the bedroom to get dressed and I fuss with my hair. I constantly appear in pictures now, and I don't look anything close to as glamorous as those finalists. I frown at my reflection. I want to be more versatile. And I want to be me. There has to be some middle ground somewhere.

I scrub the lipstick off entirely and go back to a more subdued color. The mascara and liner are fine, bulletproof stuff given to me by the makeup artist in LA. The rest of the makeup suitcase he left behind is a mystery to me — foundations, concealers, blushers, eye shadows, color correctors. I have no idea why I would ever smear yellow on my eyes or green on my cheeks.

I close the case.

Blitz returns with a siren red dress. "We should probably play it down tonight, but I can't help it. I love you in this so much."

I take the dress from him. "It's Valentine's Day!" I say. "I'm happy to wear it."

"Will you keep the bra with, you know, the hearts?" He makes random gestures toward his own chest.

"This dress is a halter, so no bra at all," I say.

He falls back against the wall. "I love it even more now."

"I can keep the white underwear, though," I say.

He closes his eyes, his hands moving to swiftly button up his charcoal shirt. "I'll think about it the whole time."

"I could take them off under the table like in that *Fifty Shades Darker* movie," I say. "I saw the clip."

Blitz claps his hands over his crotch. "Say no more or we will never make it to the restaurant."

I laugh. "Now shoo. I have to get ready in case we are seen again."

"Odds are high," he says. "But we'll do our best."

I nod and go back to the mirror. This is just the way it is. We got caught unprepared at the dance store, but this time, I'll be ready for it.

~*ˊˋ*~

Milan's is an Italian restaurant downtown near the Riverwalk. Blitz calls for Ted so we won't have to rely on the valet and can make a quick getaway if needed. He navigates the streets lined with happy couples holding hands and heading for the river.

"Good call not doing an actual Riverwalk restaurant," Ted says. "We need a place we can pull up to, and most of those require a walk to get to the entrance."

"I know," Blitz says. "We're pretty stuck for a while."

"We really need a fourth person," I say. "So Ted can stay behind the wheel and the other one can scout ahead."

Blitz laughs. "TWO bodyguards. I never thought I'd see the day."

"Well, you sort of wanted to get mobbed before," I tease.

Ted glances at us via the rearview mirror. "I'm sure the girls go nuts," he says.

"Now it's all about the rematch," I say. My phone is in my hand. I'm watching for any signs that we've been spotted. Lots of people are speculating about where we'll go. Milan's has been mentioned, but just as one of about fifty possibilities. One of them is McDonald's. I laugh.

"What?" Blitz asks.

"Somebody knows about your addiction to fast-food French fries," I say, showing him the Tweet.

"We should say I'm there," he says. "Wearing a Spurs cap. Odds are good some poor fellow will get surrounded before they figure it out."

"We'll be there in three," Ted says. "Just have to get through these two lights."

"So far, so good," Blitz says. "Man, taking you out to dinner is a major expedition these days."

"We could spend our weekends in some other city and still not miss the private lessons or the dance class," I say.

"But there's Jenica's," he reminds me.

"Oh, right." We need to train. "Any word today on what the producers are doing?"

"Nope," Blitz says. "And I don't much care. They can figure it out without me."

"Here we are," Ted says. We pull up to the valet, but Ted rolls down the front passenger window. A twenty-ish young man in a red Milan's polo shirt leans in.

"We need this couple to get in and out as inconspicuously as possible," Ted says. "There's a lot of foot traffic right here."

The guy nods, looking at the sidewalk and the people streaming by behind him. "You can take them around the block and into a small lot where the employees park. There's an entrance with a small red awning."

"Perfect," Ted says.

When the valet steps back, Ted pulls away from the curb.

"Huh," Blitz says. "Nobody told me about the private entrance last time."

"You didn't ask," Ted says.

"And you used a word with more than two syllables," Blitz says, clapping Ted on the shoulder. "You're all growed up."

Ted shakes his head. "Be nice to me or I'll Tweet your location myself."

Blitz laughs. "I always knew my antics in high school would catch up with me. But you guys are the only ones I trust these days."

Ted turns the wheel as we make the corner. "Nobody would have guessed that skinny little pipsqueak Benjamin Castillo would end up more famous than any of us."

"Just goes to show you can't count anybody out." Blitz sits back and takes my hand. "I think this is going to work," he says.

"All depends on who's inside," I say.

"It's a pretty upscale place," Blitz says.

"Blitz fans come in all shapes and bank accounts," I say.

We drive through a parking lot toward the back of the building. There are two doors. One double-wide metal delivery door, and another pretty wood door with a red awning, just like the valet told us.

"This is better," Ted says. He pulls up to the awning and hops out.

Blitz lifts the back of my hand to his lips. "You look dazzling. Here's to nobody noticing but me."

"Agreed," I say. "To quiet times and just us."

"And good food," he adds. "Your aerial stunts made me hungry."

Ted opens the door. We've just stepped out when the door beneath the awning opens. A uniformed man stands there.

"Good evening, Mr. Craven," he says. "I didn't see you on tonight's list."

"It's under Preston Rivers," Blitz says. "We've inspired a bit of a following lately."

"Understood," the man says. "Give me just a moment and we'll relocate Mr. Rivers's reservation to a more private spot in the restaurant."

"I'll be close by," Ted says and heads back to the car.

We wait on a small bench in the back corner of the restaurant. The dining area is designed for privacy, with multiple walls and large plants throughout it. After a moment, the man returns. "This way, please."

Our seat is set apart from the others, a round booth in a corner with high walls. But we do pass several tables to get to it, and it's clear several people have recognized us.

I slide into the booth. "Let's hope none of them have Twitter," I mumble as Blitz sits next to me.

"You can't get in here without a reservation. We might have people stop by, but a mob can't get to us."

I'm more rattled than I thought I would be.

Maybe we should have stayed in. But we can't hide in the hotel forever.

"Surely everyone is having their Valentine's dates and not worrying about where we are," I say.

"Sure, unless you don't have a Valentine's date and want to wreck someone else's."

The wine steward approaches and Blitz orders. The waiter brings bread, and we start to settle down. Each minute that passes makes it more likely we'll have a peaceful meal.

"This is good," Blitz says, dipping bread in olive oil and lifting it to my lips. His thumb runs along my cheek as I bite it.

Yes, this is fine. We'll be fine here. I force myself to be calm.

We order prime rib and pasta and everything we'll have to work off tomorrow. The restaurant is full of quiet murmurs and the clinking of silverware on fine china.

Dinner goes along easily and with no disruptions. We were right to come here.

The waiter has just brought us an impossibly beautiful crème brûlée to share when I feel Blitz's hand tighten around mine on the seat. "Here we go," he says.

I turn to follow his gaze.

And freeze.

It's Giselle. Holding her phone.

"Just a quick selfie," she says, leaning down to snap a quick picture of herself and Blitz.

He tries to lean away, but she's fast. I can see from the image that she's left me out.

"Giselle," Blitz says. "What are you doing here?"

"Just making sure my Valentine doesn't try to go the whole day without me!" Her voice is high and fake.

Blitz's words are low and threatening when he says, "I'm not your anything."

My face is hot and I can feel the food we just ate sitting heavily in my belly. I'm so angry I could actually stand up and punch this woman.

She stabs at her phone a moment. "You really should start using a different fake name when you get reservations. It only took my team fifteen minutes to find this one."

"Why are you even in San Antonio?" Blitz asks.

"Because you are, of course!" she says merrily. She lifts her phone again. "I'm hearing that you didn't smile in that shot. Please do better this time." She holds up her phone.

"Just stop," Blitz says. "I'm going to have you kicked out of here."

"Good luck with that," Giselle says in the false, bright voice. "I think the maître d' likes me. He did admire this dress." She stands up and turns for him, running her hands down her waist and hips. She's in a red dress too, form fitting and plunging low.

It's actually remarkably similar to mine.

She recognizes this about the same time I do. "Did Blitz pick that out for you?" Giselle asks. "His taste runs a little racy. You do seem a little innocent for the look." She clucks her tongue. "Blitz, Blitz, Blitz. You are corrupting her, aren't you?"

"That's enough, Giselle. You're not welcome."

But Giselle isn't through. She squeezes onto the seat. "Nobody's heard from you about the producer's decision. You only have a few weeks until rehearsals begin."

Blitz's jaw clenches. "I'm not taking calls right now."

I keep my mouth shut, but my mind is whirling. They made a decision? Why don't we know what it is? Normally Hannah would be here and forcing Blitz to listen to her.

"Well, your manager is trying to reach you," Giselle says. Her phone buzzes, then again, then again. She picks it up and smiles. "And your public is waiting."

I have a feeling I know what she's done. Told Twitter where we are.

"Why can't you just move on with your life?" I ask her.

Blitz tries to bite back his smile, but I can see he's pleased that I confronted her.

Gisselle swipes her finger across her screen. "Because it isn't time yet, dear. Blitz, you really need to school her on Hollywood politics." She sets the phone down on the table with a slam that startles a waitress passing by with a tray.

"I'm not interested in politics," I tell her. "We're just here having a quiet Valentine's dinner and you're ruining it."

"You know, I had a few dinners ruined by Blitz myself," Giselle says. She looks at the crème brûlée, still perfect and brown inside its lovely white and silver dish. She picks up Blitz's spoon and cracks the top. "Don't get used to having him all to yourself. He belongs to his fans."

She shoves the spoon in the dish and tries a bite. "Sugar rush," she says. "So fattening." She glances at my dress. "You better watch that figure."

With that, she slides out of the booth and flounces away, her hips swinging. A waiter stops to let her by and she blows a kiss at him.

"Great, just great," Blitz says, tossing his napkin on the table.

"Are you going to call Hannah to ask her the situation?"

"Obviously I'm still involved if I'm expected at rehearsals in a few weeks." Blitz pulls out his phone.

"And rehearsals mean dance numbers, and obviously Giselle is still in."

I reach out and wrap my fingers around his wrist. "This can all wait for tomorrow," I say. "Let's forget them for a moment."

Blitz nods and shoves his phone back in his pocket. "I can't believe she just showed up here."

"In a matching dress, no less." I'm still smarting over that.

Blitz slides his arm around me and pulls me close. "Everybody loves a red dress on Valentine's Day," he says. "I've never even seen the one she was wearing. Giselle is good at poking people where it hurts."

"You still have that naked picture of her?" I ask. "Because I have a caption or two to add myself."

Blitz smiles and kisses my forehead. "I adore you, Princess. You go straight for the jugular."

I do, I realize. That isn't good. I can't fight Giselle on her turf. She was right. I don't know anything. And I don't want to know.

Blitz waves at the waiter and pushes the spoiled crème brûlée away. "Bring us another," he says.

I press my hand to my belly. "Maybe I shouldn't."

"Are you kidding?" Blitz asks. "You are perfect." He turns to the waiter. "Bring all three desserts out."

The man nods and walks away.

Blitz drags me close to him. "I don't want you schooled in the Hollywood game. I don't want you skipping simple pleasures because somebody tries to shame you. I don't want you listening to anything but your heart."

"But you have to get back there," I say. "You'll be in LA again."

"We'll find out what they have in store for us tomorrow," Blitz says. "We've got a secret back exit out of here. A top-notch bodyguard who knows how to use *inconspicuous* in a sentence. And we have each other."

He leans in to kiss me. I know he's right. Giselle might blow up Twitter and get a chanting crowd to fill the sidewalks outside. But we have workarounds. And people on our side.

And we definitely have impenetrable, unbreakable us.

Chapter Twelve

B litz spends almost the entire next day on the phone. The producers want him to come to LA, but he refuses. He won't have anything to do with the show.

On Thursday, we head to Dreamcatcher for our private lesson with Gabriella, but we know we need to minimize our time at the academy to avoid the crowds finding us there.

So afterward, still in our dance clothes, we leave Dreamcatcher and load into Blitz's gray rental. We have agreed to return to Jenica's Dancery to work with the girl who does the aerial silks.

When we arrive at the strange building that houses the studio, Weeza is in the front room, sitting at the same makeshift cinderblock desk and giving

Blitz the same withering glare as she did the first time we came.

"I thought we got rid of you," she says. Her short blond hair is spiked up today, twisted into little points all around her head. It makes me think of a grass burr, and I giggle.

She frowns at me. "I saw you two on somebody's totally lame Facebook live broadcast. On the East Side." She stares at Blitz as if she is quite sure he doesn't have any right to visit there.

"I bet you couldn't keep your eyes off me, you little vixen," Blitz says. He reaches out to tweak her nose and she squeals with indignation. "Let's go find Jenica," Blitz says to me. "Thanks for the grand welcome," he tosses back at Weeza as we head for one of the doors.

She snorts.

"She's terrible!" I say as we enter the expansive gymnasium.

"She's definitely a piece of work," Blitz says.

We pause just inside, looking over the scene today. The aerial ropes and high mats are strung up, but unoccupied. A couple doing classical ballet occupies one corner, and two men bounce on the triad of mini-trampolines, doing front flips between them, carefully timed to avoid colliding. My stress levels rise just watching them.

Jenica is near the back wall by the barre, working

with a young woman in *pointe* shoes. I feel some chagrin at how little I've worked on my *pointe* since I advanced to them. Life has been such a whirlwind since I met Blitz.

We head her direction. She will introduce us to an instructor with experience in aerial silks.

Jenica smiles when she sees us, continuing an eight-count with the girl, who is flowing through the various positions and poses. When they pause, Jenica turns and says, "Blitz, Livia, so delighted to see you both again. And how interesting for you to seek an instructor in silks!"

"It was Livia's idea," Blitz says. "I've never done it, so it's something new. I like new."

Jenica nods. Wisps of her light brown hair have escaped her bun. She must always dress very color-fully, as today her dance leotard is a sapphire blue that fades into a bright green. The girl she teaches is traditional in pale pink.

"I'll introduce you to Bex when she arrives," Jenica says. "She's not our most punctual instructor."

Blitz and I glance at each other.

"What's her background?" Blitz asks.

"She did two years with Cirque," Jenica says. "She was an aerialist. Then she got pregnant and took a break. Now she teaches. We don't have a lot of call for it. Not many places can host an aerialist, and there isn't a lot of work for it."

"We're just doing it for fun," Blitz says.

Jenica reaches over and squeezes his bicep. "You've been increasing your weights," she says. "You still interested in lifts?"

"I am," he says. "But we're going to focus on this for a while. See how it feels."

Jenica's eyes focus on something behind us. "Oh, there she is." She waves. "Bex! Over here!"

A woman with dark hair and long legs strides over to us. She has a pile of fabric over one arm. "Hello," she says shyly, looking at Blitz like she can't believe he's in front of her. "This was a surprise."

Blitz spreads his hands. "I'm just a dancer looking for some help with a new skill."

Bex nods. "And you're Livia. I saw you on the show. You just started *pointe*?"

"Yes," I say. "I'd only had my toe shoes a couple weeks at that point."

"You're brave," she says.

"I'll leave you all to it," Jenica says. She turns to count the ballerina back in.

Blitz, Bex, and I head to the corner where the fall of blue silk flutters.

"We have a good setup here," Bex says. "It isn't easy to find a space with room for aerial work."

"The ceiling is really high," I say.

"Yes," Bex says. "And there is enough room for these giant mats." She pats the cushioned stairs, each one at least two feet high, that rise above our head. "It's really important to be able to get the height you need when it's time to learn drops."

I look up to see how high I would be for a drop, and my belly rolls over. This seems very different from the small maneuvers I did from the canopy of the bed.

"So, the basics," Bex says. "It takes a special kind of fabric for this work." She holds out the black cloth in her hand. "It can't stretch, and either it must have some texture for your grip, or you need to use rosin to give you some stickiness."

I touch her fabric. It feels a lot like the one I bought.

She sets it down and leads us over to the lengths that hang from a bar attached to the rafters. "Here we have a swivel, but sometimes you simply work with a single piece of cloth tossed over a bar." She shrugs. "It doesn't matter from a grip and hold stand-point, but if you can spin, it adds a lot to the drama. Most aerialists work on a swivel. Since we need two, we'll just toss a second set over."

Bex unfolds the fabric partway and tosses it over her shoulder. Then she deftly climbs the silks, wrap-ping her foot, standing up, and moving her foot up the silk. "This is called a French Climb," she says, "or Basic Climb, to some."

When she reaches the swivel at the top, she wraps

the silks around her ankles and tosses the fabric over the rafter a few feet away.

"We will start easy," she says, sliding down the silk like it's a fireman's pole. "Basic wrist lock, foot lock, box stand, and hip hold." She lands on the floor mat next to us. "But first, we warm up."

She takes us through push-ups, crunches, and stretches to make sure our arms, core, and legs are ready for the work. I've been trying to build up my arm strength, but as I gaze up the length of the silks, I wonder if I have done enough.

Bex leads us over to the silks. "We're going to start with a climb so I get a feel for your strength and agility as we get started."

She shows us how to wrap the silk around our ankles and how to hold the fabric. Then she jumps down.

"Let's see what you can do."

Blitz wraps his black silk and starts up, his arm muscles bulging as he moves.

I swallow hard. I can do this. It was my idea. I just never climbed the silk before, since I had so little room. My hands grasp the blue silk and I turn my foot around the tail end.

"Remember to flex your feet for now," Bex says. "Later, when we do extensions and poses, you might point like in ballet, but for now, flexing is for safety and to keep the silk where you want it."

I nod to acknowledge her instruction and push up. This first one is easy, so I hang on to the silk as I unwrap the fabric and bend my leg to wrap it again higher up.

Blitz has already mastered it and is halfway to the top. "Now this is cool," he says, looking down at me.

"If you feel fatigue, come on down," she says. "You can slide or just climb in reverse."

I pull myself up a second time. I feel like I've gotten nowhere, still only a few feet above the ground. I swing precariously for a second, and struggle to keep my hold as my feet move out from under me.

Bex grabs me and steadies me back in an upright position. "Use your core," she says. "Keep it tight so you stay straight. Try not to bend your arms. Keep your wrapped foot flexed."

Too many things!

I reach higher, release my leg, then wrap it again, trying to stay flexed. I can already feel my arms getting tired. I place my free foot on top of the wrapped one, and stand up. I'm a little farther up now.

Again, reach up, lift legs, and stand again. I'm figuring out how to do it without stressing my arms so much. After a couple more climbs, I'm also halfway up. I look over at Blitz's silks.

He's reached the top and is standing on the silk. He waves at me. "This is off the hook," he says.

I want to be at the top with him, but I make the mistake of looking down. I instantly lose my balance, my foot swinging out again. I clutch the silks, but my arms start to shake right away since I'm clinging rather than standing.

And Bex is too far below to steady me.

I feel panic taking over.

"You're all right," Bex calls up. "Use your core, straighten out, get your feet below you."

Blitz starts to come down. My arms are burning as I try to hold on while frantically trying to pull my body back to vertical.

"You can do it, Princess," Blitz says. He's even with me now. "Lean forward."

I do what he says and feel my chest moving over my legs. Then the blessed feeling of my weight settling on my feet again.

"Straighten your arms," Bex calls. "It keeps you from clinging and using your weaker muscles."

I finally feel confident enough to let go of one silk and lift one arm higher, then the other. Now there is no weight on my arms, only my legs.

"You got it," Blitz says. "Let's go down together."

I watch him squat down, then unwrap his leg, lower it, then rewrap it with a straight body.

I do the same, scooting down like an inchworm, until I'm close enough to the ground to jump off.

"That was good," Bex says. "Let's do a few ballistic stretches and then I want you to jump right in and do it again. No fear."

What? Again? I look up at the silks. Tendrils of unease uncurl in my belly as I remember how I got stuck.

"She's right," Blitz says. "You have to train your brain not to feel fear."

He knows I'm afraid. I manage to give him a weak smile, and clap my hands against my opposite shoulders in a bear hug, out and in, until I feel less shaky.

"Let's do it," Bex says. But as soon as I'm a couple body lengths up, I notice she moves one of the tall mats closer to us, as if she isn't positive I'll make it this time.

This punches my determination into gear. The climb isn't hard on my arms as long as I stay over my feet. I work carefully as I bend, wrap, lift, and unwrap to avoid getting off balance or swinging.

Still, I don't quite make it to the top. When my arms and thighs start quivering, I go ahead and make my way back to the floor. Blitz is faster and makes it to the top and ends up touching down the same time I do.

"This is wicked," Blitz says. "What do we do next?"

Bex shows us the foot lock, where we tie our foot into the silks so we can do different poses securely. Then the knot, which is the basis for many of the positions, from the box stand to rolling drops.

After an hour of this, I feel more spent than anything I've ever done in ballet. I want to lie on the ground and never move again, but Blitz is completely jazzed. So I stay on the mat and watch as he and Bex climb the ropes. She shows him how to spin, and they twirl in tandem, suspended in the air.

This motivates me to get my butt back up there. Bex slides down and suggests Blitz get a little lower. Then I get in a foot lock and bend over, the silks between my thighs, one arm outstretched until I'm horizontal on my side. The silk holds me up by the hip, and from there, Bex turns me to start the spin.

Blitz drops down to watch. "That is absolutely gorgeous," he says. "Too bad nobody will ever see us do them."

"You could always join the circus," Bex says.

I slide down. "Do you miss it?" I ask.

"Cirque?" she asks. "Sure. It's a rush. But it's also four hundred shows a year. The wear and tear on your body is incredible. It's not something you can sustain for long." She tugs on the black silk to start bringing it down. I guess today's lesson is over.

"How did you get in?" Blitz asks.

"It's a process," Bex says. "There are auditions a

few times a year around the world. Some people are scouted. The cuts are merciless. Often only a handful will make it through out of hundreds."

"Dang," Blitz says.

"And that only gets you into the training academy, where they will make more cuts. Medical is severe. You have to be top notch, and no braces or accommodations. Then you have to get a contract, and not everyone does. They keep a database of talent and only cast people when they need them."

Blitz nods. "I'm probably already too old," he says.

Bex laughs. "For acrobatic work, yes. But it's not your background."

"Wouldn't be my thing anyway," Blitz says.

"No," Bex says. "It takes very strict dedication."

Blitz puts his hand over his heart. "I'm wounded to think you believe I'm not dedicated."

Bex laughs. "Your reputation precedes you."

Blitz takes my hand. "Well, that whole lifestyle is behind me. We're doing this for fun."

"You can come back tomorrow," Bex says. "Or give your arms a recovery day. Let me know."

"We will," Blitz says. "Thank you."

Bex nods, folding up the silks. We pick up our bags.

Jenica heads toward us as we move toward the door. "Blitz," she says, "you sure you don't want to do more work today? You've only just warmed up!"

Blitz winks at me, and I remember how he felt about Jenica's work schedules. Too much, too high risk for injury.

"We're good for today," he says. "I'm needed back at my hotel." He tugs his phone out of the side of his bag, glances at it, and shoves it back in. "Thirty minutes ago, apparently." He sighs.

"What's going on?" I ask.

"I'll tell you in the car," Blitz says.

"See you again soon," Jenica calls. "You can schedule more time with Weeza on the way out if you would like."

Blitz laughs. "I think she'd delete anything I book. I'll have my assistant arrange things."

Jenica waves and we head past the scowling Weeza.

"Miss you already," Blitz says as we pass.

We hurry through the door and out to the gray car before she can insult us again.

Chapter Thirteen

Blitz seems tense as we drive back to the hotel.

"So what's going on?" I ask him.

His jaw is set, and he doesn't answer right away. I reach out and squeeze his arm.

He puts his hand over mine. "My lawyer Larry flew in from LA this morning," he says. "He's at the hotel."

"What?" I ask. "I thought you got someone local when you needed things done here in San Antonio."

"This is big," he says. "The executive producers of *Dance Blitz* filed a lawsuit against me. They probably had it ready to go, and when I refused them again yesterday, they filed it."

My heart drops. "Bennett too?" I assume Danika didn't know, as we talked to her at Dreamcatcher this morning. Or maybe she wasn't supposed to say anything. I don't know how any of this works.

"He probably tried to stop it, but there's only so much he can do. He's only one of four executive producers."

"Who are the others?" I try to picture the room at the last meeting, but we hadn't stayed long. "I remember the red-faced man who threatened to sue."

"That's Lance," Blitz says. "He's been having a fling with Giselle, or something. She's got him under her spell. That's clear."

"And there was a woman."

"Yes, Taya. Then Bennett. Then a man named Drake Addler. He was quiet."

"What will happen?"

"I guess Larry will tell us." His face is grim as he exits the freeway near the hotel. "You want to go up and change first? He's already been here an hour."

"No, we shouldn't keep him waiting," I say.

"Probably not."

We pull up to the hotel and the valet opens my door. I feel hot and sick. It's finally come to this. I wonder now if I should have saved Blitz during the live finale after all. If he was going to walk away, maybe it should have been with them firing him. Then we wouldn't be here.

The ride up in the elevator feels long. Blitz holds my hand. I fiddle with my leotard self-consciously.

We don't go all the way up to the floor with our suite, but one about halfway. When we step out, there is a lounge like ours, but bigger, with more people. We pass by it and on to a hall where the doors are all open. They are meeting rooms.

Blitz checks his phone again and pauses in front of one of the doors to peek in. "Found him."

The room would hold about forty people normally and has a speaker podium at the front. There's a round table near the back. A man in a pale gray suit and a woman in a black dress sit at it, chatting. They stand up when we enter.

"Blitz, Livia," Larry says. "Glad we could get together."

"You came all the way from LA," Blitz says. "It's bound to be important."

Larry's face sobers. "It is. You two sit down."

The chairs are round and cushioned. I set my bag on the ground by my feet and fold my hands on my lap. I know this isn't about me directly, but I'm nervous. Blitz is right, Larry wouldn't have flown here himself, no doubt canceling other important meetings, if it wasn't critical they meet.

"Just hit me with it," Blitz says. "No sugarcoating."

Larry opens a folder and turns it around to slide it across the polished wood table. "You were served a breach of contract lawsuit at close of business yesterday," Larry says. "I did a quick review and booked a flight because if you're going to fight this, we need a strategy. It's not pretty. It goes for the jugular, that you knowingly and maliciously corrupted the holdings of the producers, causing them financial harm."

Blitz's face is like stone as he flips through a few pages. "This is legal mumbo jumbo," he says, pushing it back. "What's the upshot?"

"They are seeking damages," he says. "Big ones. I'm not privy to your holdings, but you're going to want to settle out of court. Their numbers are meant to scare you."

"Where are they?" Blitz asks.

Larry flips a few pages. I look with him. There are more zeros there than I can quickly add up. But it's millions of dollars. Millions.

Blitz's face is still calm. "Did you put in a call to Bennett?"

"Yes, but his lawyer is keeping him at bay. He's not going to fraternize on this. You know he can't."

"What do they want me to do?" he asks.

"The show," Larry says. "They want the three original bonus shows, on a rush schedule to appease the network and their advertisers. And two more shows to round out the eliminations of the three finalists plus Livia."

"They want me to consider those other girls?" Blitz asks.

I can see the tension in his shoulders.

"The particulars are not in the document," he says. "They just have listed the three contracted shows that were promoted but never filmed, plus two option shows, also in the contract, which, honestly, is less than they could go for. They could ask for another fifteen-show season. You could get out of that, but the non-compete clause requires you do no other dance shows for five years if you do."

"So they really only have me on the hook for three shows I skipped out on. I don't care about the five year lockout."

"Yes, they have you on the hook for three. But the malice is what gives them leverage. They feel like they can prove you purposefully destroyed your image to end the show." Larry closes the folder and sits back. "No way we'd go to trial on that. It would be a circus you don't need." He glances my way and my cheeks burn. I know he's thinking about Gabriella, and the near-disaster we had with Denham, her birth father.

"I will not be bullied into doing that show. It was only a hit because of me," Blitz says.

"That's a cocky attitude and why we have to settle," Larry says, his voice calm and even. "They know you."

"If I don't do it, it's what, just a money issue?"

"Yes, but these damages are ridiculous. It's over

the budget of the show. I know you weren't paid anything near that. You couldn't have been."

"I can do commercials or whatever," Blitz says. "They are not going to force my hand."

"Blitz, you knew those shows were coming. You did the promo for them." Larry's voice has taken on a soothing quality. The woman in the black dress quietly types their discussion. "Just do them."

"They will crucify Livia," Blitz says. "She is not under contract. This is straight-up blackmail."

"This is straight-up you not holding up your end of a contract," Larry says. "I'll fight this if you want me to. I'll let you go bankrupt. I'll let you be a Hollywood pariah. But you need to ask yourself if it's worth it over a few weeks of shooting and a couple dance numbers."

Blitz looks up at the ceiling. I follow his gaze. It's pretty, actually, little metal squares with patterns on them, all lined up.

I decide it's time for me to speak up. "Let's do the show, Blitz," I say. "You get to pick the winner. It's not like you're going to have to propose to anyone. So what if I can't dance as well as them?"

Blitz turns to me, his dark eyes soft. "Princess, you have no idea what you're about to get into. Brutal Tweets dissecting your every move, what you eat, what you say, comparing you to the other girls, deciding whether or not we should be together."

I pull my cell phone out of my bag. I flip it on, find the Twitter app, and click the little "x" in the corner. The phone confirms, "App deleted."

"Next problem?" I say.

"Paparazzi. Fans. You can't go anywhere," he argues.

"Please," I say. "We're already dealing with that. It will die down after the episodes air."

"They'll make me go on dates with those other girls. I'll have to act like they have a chance. You'll have to go through that." His eyes are more somber.

"I already watched you buy a diamond ring for one of them," I say. "It's a role. It's acting. I'll be cheering you on, and heck, maybe I will be the first one to say you sure don't seem very into that Mariah girl."

Blitz looks from me to Larry back to me. Seconds tick by. I keep my expression as neutral as possible. I'm scared to death, of course I am. But if Larry is acting like this, then we have to listen.

"All right," Blitz says. "Tell them I'm on board." He taps the table. "It's your job to get me out after these five episodes. Seriously. Your job. After this, I'm done."

Larry nods. "I'll let them know. I'm sure they will be in touch with a production schedule." He tucks the folders away. "You're doing the right thing. Nobody wins when this happens. Just do your time.

Put on that smile. Hang on to your girl. Muddle through."

He stands up. We do too, and shake his hand.

"Pleasure to meet you in person, Livia. I'm glad your personal matters are resolved."

I nod at him.

The girl packs up her laptop. We head to the hallway and part ways, them to the regular elevator, us to the private one.

And just like that, we're back in the world of *Dance Blitz*.

Chapter Fourteen

Hannah calls that afternoon. Blitz sends her call to voice mail, then phones his assistant Shelly to deal with her and get the details of the production schedule. Neither of us feel any love for his manager. When the show is over, she is too.

We sit on our balcony, watching the sun set on the San Antonio skyline. It probably won't be long before we have to go to LA.

Blitz scans some of the messages coming through and sighs.

"I'm actually going to miss this hotel," he says. "But we're going to be gone almost three months. We should pack our things."

I nod. "We have a lot."

"I'll have a service do it. Where would you like to live while we're in LA? A hotel like this? A condo? My place is still full of cameras. We'll only go there when we're contracted to do so."

"The hotels feel safe," I say. "But I would like to be able to cook a little. Feel like something is mine."

"I'll have Shelly send us some properties. I don't think I'll buy another one, just rent something. You don't want to live permanently in LA, right? We'll come back here for Gabriella."

I nod, my voice feeling thick. "We'll have to tell her we're going to be gone for a while."

"We'll do the wheelchair class on Tuesday and let them know then."

My head falls back against the chair. It's cool out, and the tear that squeezes out of my eye feels chilly by the time it slips down my cheek.

We get the schedule the next day. Rehearsals are supposed to start on Monday, but Blitz insists we will arrive Tuesday night. They agree to delay until Wednesday.

We spend part of Friday with Bex at Jenica's, working on more aerial silks. When she hears we're leaving town next week, she gives us the name of another instructor in LA. There's a lot of them there, and some specialty trainers in Vegas if we need help with particular moves. I know we probably won't have time for it. But everything is temporary. We just have to get through the five shows.

We pack some of our things over the weekend,

the items we want to take with us ourselves. Bennett offers his plane on Tuesday, saying nothing about the lawsuit or the result. We accept.

Soon there is nothing left but good-byes. I know they aren't forever, but it's still a big change. I've never lived anywhere but Texas and have only spent a few days here and there in LA.

I haven't made up with my parents, who still won't speak to me.

And there's Gabriella. I won't see her for months.

Blitz has new ribbon sticks made for the class, ones they can take home. Each stick is the girl's favorite color, all made from the same type of sheer shiny fabric. It touches me that he knows each of them so well.

We place the girls in a semicircle at the start of class and Blitz passes out the sticks. He talks a little about each girl and her strengths as a dancer.

When he gets to Gabriella, my heart clenches. I take pictures with my phone, glad for an occasion to get really good, close shots without revealing how important she is to me.

"You, our spunky dark-haired queen," Blitz says, "have a smile that will light up the stage and a passion that makes every dance of yours something extra special. Everyone who sees you will know that dance is the thing you love most in the world." He hands her an emerald green ribbon stick.

Like the rest of the girls, tears are streaming down her face. She hiccups, trying to say something, but instead just buries her face on his shoulder when he hugs her. I know how she feels. That shoulder is the best.

Janel brings the music tempo up after that, and we have a good time rolling around the room, free dancing and doing conga lines. When the lights blink to signal the end of class, the girls clutch their new ribbon sticks and roll over to say their good-byes.

I focus in on Gabriella. She's holding up better than she did an hour ago, watching Blitz with bright, sad eyes. "I will miss you," she says to Blitz. Then she turns to me. "You too, Miss Livie."

When her gaze meets mine, it takes everything in me not to lose it. I bend down to hug her, and she clings to me. It's the longest embrace we've ever had, and I revel in the feel of her, the strawberry shampoo, her slight little figure bending forward in the wheelchair.

She is the most precious thing I have.

The next class starts to trickle in, and the moms arrive to escort out the reluctant dancers. Blitz and I hang back, watching them all leave. He squeezes my hand.

When Janel has started the new class, we pick up our bags and head out into the hall. Only moms are outside, chatting or watching through the windows.

A few glance over at Blitz, but nobody says anything. We're lucky nobody here gives up our location.

"One more time in the storage room?" Blitz asks.

I nod, looking down the hall as if Gabriella will appear again, although she's surely gone by now.

He leads me to the back wall and through the door of the storage room. It always feels magical to me to come here, light slanting through the high windows. It lands in fine beams on the mats, equipment, and costumes stored here. A round cap sparkles over the edge of a box, a jaunty feather coming off one side.

"Time for a montage," Blitz says merrily. He leads me behind a rack and takes on the voice of an announcer. "Right here in this spot, Blitz Craven first kissed the young and lovely Livia, catching her by surprise." He pulls me close and presses a gentle kiss on my lips.

Then he twirls me out, making me laugh. "And on this wall right here…" He lifts me up, turns in a circle, and sets me down next to a blank spot by the shelves. "The less innocent Livia wrapped her naughty, naughty legs around the wayward dance star."

He lifts my legs so they encircle his hips.

I speak up next. "And then the clumsy wannabe ballerina knocked over a box of shakers, and the secretive couple was discovered by a fellow instructor."

Blitz laughs. "I forgot about that."

He wraps his arms around me and turns, holding me up against him. My hair flies out. "This has been a wonderful place for us, and I promise you." His face gets earnest, his lips in a serious line. "We will come back here. Together."

My breath hitches. I want to think our love will not be in question. That we'll weather everything that is about to happen. But when I am admitting things to myself, I know this is going to be a hard road. It will be everything Blitz said. A social media storm. A barrage of criticism and scrutiny.

"I believe in us," I tell him. "We're going to do this."

He holds me close. "We're going to rock it."

I have to believe him.

Chapter Fifteen

Bennett isn't on the plane that takes us to LA that afternoon. Blitz hasn't talked to him about the show, but it doesn't matter anyway. We're committed to this course.

I get to meet his assistant Shelly the moment we land. She's waiting on the tarmac with Duke and a different car, an enormous black SUV.

She's very tiny, not even five feet tall, and extremely petite with bright pink hair cut short around her pixie-like face. She wears jeans and a black tank top that says "Bite me." A dozen gold hoops line one of her earlobes.

She isn't what I expected at all.

"I have three properties for you to visit for a rental," she says, "but I don't see any time in your schedule to go look. Rehearsals start at eight in the morning and you will literally have no time to do anything, as the first show will be shot in three weeks."

Duke waves at us, making a "talkie talkie" motion with his hands as he follows Shelly with our bags. And it's true. Shelly doesn't so much as take a breath as we load into the SUV.

"We're going to keep you as quiet as possible," Shelly says as we sit down. She gets in the front next to Duke and twists around. "That's why we got this car. Duke isn't to take out your Jag unless it's an official event. I'm taking your request seriously to blow off Hannah and avoid any unnecessary publicity."

Blitz is about to say something, but she charges on.

"Since you didn't want to go to your condo, I made reservations at the Ritz. They know you are coming and that your privacy is of utmost concern. They have you keyed in for the rear entrance and a secure floor. We couldn't get any presidential suites because, well, this is Hollywood, but it's a nice big room. I hope to get you in a rental by the weekend. Maybe I can pick one if you don't get a chance to look."

"Shelly! Stop!" Blitz says. "Hello! I want you to meet Livia."

"Hello, Livia," Shelly says. "I already know your dress size and shoe size. I have a ballet instructor lined up for you. We all assumed you would continue your studies. Let us know if that changes. The choreographer wants to meet with you first thing and the two of you will need to dance for everyone so we can fit your style into the show."

Blitz shakes his head. "What Shelly is trying to say is 'Hello, nice to meet you too.'"

Shelly waves off his comment. "She'll get used to me." She flips through screens on her phone and goes on.

"Hannah is not pleased to have me as a go-between, but I told her to suck it. Here was her response." She holds up her phone, where a message has been zoomed in on. It reads "You. Are. Unprofessional."

She turns the phone back to look at it herself. "I took that as a compliment, coming from her." She sighs. "Any questions?"

Blitz and I look at each other and laugh. "I think you've covered it."

"Oh, meals," Shelly says. "Your chef got here yesterday and will prepare everything for both of you to eat while on the set each day. He said, and I quote, 'Do not let him go to McDonald's.'"

Blitz leans forward in his seat. "Duke, you know what that means."

"I'm on it," Duke says. He turns on his signal.

"Are you heading to McDonald's?" Shelly asks, her voice exasperated.

"Of course he is," Blitz says. "Livia, quarter pounder or double Mac?"

I giggle. "You know I won't eat that stuff."

"And you were so close to being the perfect girl," he says, lifting my hand to kiss my fingers.

"Enjoy your last night of freedom," Shelly says. "Because starting tomorrow, you are owned by *Dance Blitz*."

"Just for five episodes," Blitz says.

"It's going to be different," Shelly says. "It's already different. Those finalists are feeling their power. They are calling more shots. And they don't listen to me as well as they did Hannah. You might want to bring her back."

Blitz shrugs. "It doesn't matter. I choose the winner in the end. It's pointless for them to force my hand."

Shelly and Duke exchange glances.

"What?" Blitz asks. "Surely nobody thinks I'm going to choose anyone but Livia."

"I'm going to pull over for this one," Duke says. He turns into the parking lot of a pharmacy and shifts the car into park.

My belly quivers a little. This must be big.

Shelly tugs on a piece of her pink hair, her lips twisted. "They changed the format of the show," she says. "You weren't here yesterday for the kickoff meeting, since you insisted on arriving today."

"What is the new format?" Blitz asks.

Shelly reaches into an oversized bag and pulls out a sheaf of papers. "These are the roughs," she says. "They outline the five episodes."

The first page has five paragraphs labeled S3 E1 to E5. I guess it stands for season three, and episodes one through five.

I've only read a couple lines about the first episode being based on four dates, when Blitz flings it to the floor. "Nobody said ANYTHING about doing a live weekly!" he says.

"The live format for the finale was really popular," she says. "And it's the best way to get big numbers on the audience vote since they are short on publicity due to the quick timeline. They are trying to salvage the original release dates."

"It's a live show again?" I ask.

Blitz nods and covers his eyes with his hand for a moment, struggling to control his anger.

"We can do that," I say. "We did it before."

"That's not the real rub," Duke says. "You're missing the point."

I look from Blitz to Shelly to Duke. "What are you talking about?"

"The new format is so they can do live voting," Shelly explains. "It's not up to Blitz to choose this time. This winner will be determined by the TV audience."

_*´`*_

I SINK BACK AGAINST THE SEAT. BLITZ'S FACE IS hard and angry. "Who authorized this without my input?" he demands.

"You'll have to talk to the execs," Shelly says. "I think under the new agreement, the one that you signed to avoid the lawsuit, the format is no longer under your control."

"You told Larry to get you off the show after five," I say. "This is probably what he had to do."

Duke pulls out of the parking lot. "Still Micky D's?" he asks.

"Forget it," Blitz says. "I want to get to the hotel and make some calls."

He's as stormy as I've ever seen him. I'm anxious too. I know my dancing isn't nearly at the level of the other girls. The audience will be unforgiving. I'll be voted off the first show.

I reach down and pick up the sheaf of papers again, trying to puzzle out what will happen.

Episode 1 is called "Meet the Dates." It doesn't have any dance numbers. And it's not live either. Blitz will go on four dates, one with each of the three finalists and one with me, and clips will be aired along with the host, who will talk to the audience about the girls. No one will be eliminated.

Episode 2 is the first live show. It's called "Slow Dance." There's a dance number with each girl, and Blitz will do interviews about each of us as a partner, plus interview spotlights on each of us. Callers will vote during the show and up to two hours after.

Episode 3 is called "Classic Dance." All four of us do a dance with Blitz, interspersed with interviews and rehearsal footage. The votes from Episode 2 will be revealed and the girl who was eliminated does a "Final Dance" with Blitz.

Episode 4 is "Sexy Dance." Same format. Another girl goes in the end.

In the last episode, the competition will be down to two girls, both showing the unique dance style they have developed with Blitz. Previous dancers from earlier in the series will do numbers with Blitz, reliving some of the moments that were iconic to the show. I scan and note that the sexy bed scene is only shown as a clip. That girl wasn't invited back.

These dances are just for fun, because the audience has already decided on the winner based on the sexy dance episode. The winner is announced at the end.

At least there is no wedding proposal scripted in. They didn't go that far.

I roll up the papers and tap my palm anxiously as the streets of LA roll by. It will be dark soon, and before I know it, we'll be up and at the studio.

I guess some of us will be in rehearsals while others are out filming the dates. I don't know how all that will work. I turn to look at Blitz. He's staring out the window, still scowling. I understand how he feels. The show he built on his charisma and craziness is no longer his. And he wants this triumphant ending with the two of us, and it just got snatched away.

I reach across the seat and hold on to his wrist. "You okay, Blitz?"

Shelly glances back anxiously, then turns away.

Blitz blows out a long hard gush of air. "This business sucks," he says. "Nobody's in it for anything but ratings. Everybody has to cover their ass."

"We'll be fine," I tell him. "It's just television. Maybe I'll get crazier than you and have an onscreen fling with Giselle myself."

Duke has a coughing fit and Shelly hammers him on the back. Blitz just shakes his head.

"You're really something," he says, dragging me across the seat closer to him.

"I could kiss a girl. Maybe I'd like it," I say.

Duke chokes out another cough.

"Your lips are mine," Blitz says. "She doesn't deserve them." He leans in and kisses me, and I can feel his body relax.

"I really think you two are going to do fine," Shelly says. "Everybody loves a true romance. And the other girls just didn't cut it."

I look up at Blitz. For his sake, and okay, maybe for mine too, I hope she's right.

Chapter Sixteen

The next morning, Duke picks us up in the black SUV. Shelly isn't with him. I'm dressed in plain workout clothes, same as Blitz. I have no idea what to expect.

Duke passes Blitz an Egg McMuffin. "Since you skipped the Golden Arches last night."

Blitz takes it with a grimace. I know how he feels. I don't want to eat anything greasy or heavy, unsure of what I'll be put through today, and for how long. At least Blitz knows all the people involved.

Duke is cheerful and feeling chatty. He asks, "So that Giselle chick is still around? What is going on with her? Can't she take a hint?"

Blitz stares out his side window.

"Come on, as soon as I got that message from you

that night, I figured she was toast!" Duke glances in the rearview mirror at us.

This gets Blitz's attention. "You actually got that picture?"

"Sure," he says. "I figured you sent it to everybody when it went viral. I sure as hell didn't show it to anybody. You split town, so we never talked about it."

"It got posted to Twitter."

"Yeah, I saw that," Duke says. "It's like it went two places at once. Doesn't make sense."

"No, it doesn't," Blitz says. "But I checked my phone that day. I'd sent it from my phone, straight to Twitter."

"How much did you have to drink, *compadre*?" he asks. "Were you three sheets to the wind?"

"More than usual," Blitz admits. "I was sick of that girl and booze got me through it."

I stay quiet through this exchange. I rarely see Blitz drink more than a cocktail or a glass of wine at client meetings. We had a bar in our hotel room for months, and he almost never poured anything from it.

"Something is definitely fishy about that," Duke says.

"Water under the bridge now," Blitz says.

We pull up to the giant gates of the studio and are stopped by a guard. Duke flashes him a pass and we're waved through.

My head feels light and jangly with nerves. I try to focus on my happy memories here. The prop room and the satin bed. The end of the live finale, when we escaped with Bennett and Juliet.

I wish I had brought my blue-sprayed toe shoes. I keep them in a special box, not to be worn since that epic night. They might have brought me luck today.

Duke pulls up to the double doors of the building. "Have fun, lovebirds. Blitz, don't punch anybody. Livia, if you kiss any girls, send pictures." He winks at me.

Duke jumps out to open my door. Blitz meets me on the other side.

Blitz waves Duke off, and we enter the familiar hall.

The activity is more than I expected. A man pushes a rack of costumes down the corridor. Two men with headsets chat as they hurry through a door. Three girls in leotards spot Blitz and wave wildly, eyes big.

Blitz takes my hand. "Come on," he says. "Let's see where we're supposed to go."

We head into the viewing room I first entered when I arrived months ago with Bennett. The place is crowded with people, some in suits, others in dance gear. I quickly spot the three finalists, Mariah, Christy, and Giselle. They are dressed the same as I am, and I let out a sigh that I got that much right.

"Look who decided to show up finally," Giselle says. "I wondered if we were all going to be competing for a ghost."

Blitz's manager Hannah steps forward, as casual as I've ever seen her in jeans and a gray sweater. "I know you're not speaking to me, but legal needs Livia to sign all the documents that allow her on the show." She points to the same man I saw the night of the finale, when Bennett signed on my behalf. "Right over there."

I nod and let go of Blitz. I'm not going to even worry about the papers. Whatever they say I have to do, I will do. None of this is about me. It's about getting to the end of the show and returning to our lives.

I sit in the chair opposite the man. He extends a hand. "Nice to see you again, Livia," he says. "I'm Liam Reynolds."

"I remember," I say. "Where do I need to sign?"

"You want to go over these?" he asks. "They contractually obligate you to do season three of *Dance Blitz*, five episodes or until you are eliminated from the competition."

"I know," I say. "And nothing that happens to me due to the show is part of your liability, et cetera, et cetera."

He grins at that. "We should review your financial data, when and how you will be paid, residuals, and your points toward sales of subsequent media after the show is over."

I didn't realize I would be paid. But of course I would. I'm not married to Blitz. I'm my own person. And I'm working for a show.

"Okay," I say.

Liam flips through to the last pages. "This is the amount you will make per episode. Here are subsidiary properties, such as media sales, promotional spots, and endorsements related to the franchise. Merchandising is separate, if your likeness is used on things such as lunch boxes or dolls." His pen touches several charts.

I feel like I can't be seeing this right. No wonder the finalists fought for this. I wouldn't make this much money in years and years, no matter what I was qualified to do. I could pay for college.

I could buy my own car. My own house.

I'm too shocked to speak.

"I take it these numbers are adequate for you," Liam says. "We should get you an agent. I think Bennett has had someone make sure you were part of the appropriate guilds and unions to work. I'll double-check on that, as we can't pay you until all that is square."

"Thank you," I say and pick up the pen.

"Don't thank me," Liam says. "You need someone in your corner looking out for your interests. This is a short-term contract with standard rates and no add-on clauses. Bennett saw to that. But whatever you do next will need an experienced hand."

I scrawl my name and initial in all the spots he indicates.

"The things I'm doing next won't require any expertise," I say. "I'll teach little ballerinas and keep Blitz out of trouble."

"That's a big job for sure," Liam says. He shakes my hand again. "Now I believe that young woman over there needs you."

I turn and see the choreographer who was none too pleased to see me at the live finale of the show. She's willowy, like a dancer, her brown hair pulled up in a tight bun. Her eyebrows are dramatic arches, and one lifts higher than the other as she sees me approaching.

"I'm Amara," she says. "And you're still here. That's something."

"Hello," I say uncertainly.

"Blitz is on the set with Mariah right now," she says. "We'll do a warm-up in another room, and then I'll watch the two of you together. I hope you've been dancing since the December finale. We need you to be competition ready in three weeks."

I'm not sure I could be competition ready in a year, but I follow her out of the viewing room and down the hall. We stop a few doors down, past the dressing room. Everything is unlocked today, and Amara leads us into a studio with a mirrored wall. Mats are stacked along the side.

Two other girls are here, chorus dancers, by the looks of them. Their eyes cut at me as we enter, then they return to their stretches.

"Follow my lead," Amara says. She takes me through a thorough set of warm-ups, enough to make me feel a little fatigued by the time a half hour has passed. Partway through, the other girls leave.

"I won't be doing this for you every day," Amara says. "But I'm here now to ensure that you understand the rigor of what you are about to do and to be adequately prepared for each day's dancing. While you and Blitz are filming your parts of the first show, we'll also be rehearsing numbers for the live episodes."

"What if I'm sent home after the first one?" I ask.

"Confident, aren't you?" Amara's voice is cutting. "We focus on the next dance, and just prepare the basics for the future. But we have to be ready, as time will fly once all this begins."

I snatch up my bag as she hurries out of the room. I assume I'm supposed to follow her. This woman doesn't do anything at a normal pace.

The door bangs my elbow as I simultaneously try to go through it and pull a water bottle out of my bag. Amara turns at the clang and says, "Don't get injured. We have no protocol for what to do with a hurt finalist."

I rub my elbow as we head toward the stage doors. They're propped open today, and I can hear voices and music inside.

Unlike the night of the finale, the backstage area is brightly lit. Quite a lot of people stand around.

"Jessie, you're on Livia," Amara says. "Keep her hydrated and do what she asks."

A young girl with wispy blond hair, barely sixteen, hurries over with the easy grace of a dancer. She wears all black, like the crew did the night of the show, which I assume means she is backstage help.

"Hello, Livia," she says, her voice a squeak. "I'll hold on to your bag." She takes it from me. "I'll be your gopher. If you need something to eat, or to get a prop or dance shoes or anything, I'm the one who does it for you."

"Thank you, Jessie," I say. "Are you a dancer?"

"I want to be," she says. "I was about to start in the corps at a ballet company until this happened." She points at her ankle, which is wrapped in a bandage. "I got this job so I can at least do something until I'm cleared to dance again."

"Does it hurt?" I can't imagine losing my dream to an injury.

"Not really. It's just not up to the dance work I need to do to stay in the company. They won't risk it.

I'm not worth the risk." She says this very matter-of-factly, as if it is just part of life.

"I'm really sorry, Jessie."

"This is fun. I'm lucky." She waves to the stage. "They are still working."

The music has stopped. When I look beyond the stage wings, I see Blitz lowering Mariah out of a lift. She has on a wispy skirt now. Amara is shaking her head.

"I should have been out here," she says. "That was completely wrong."

Conflicting feelings of relief that someone besides me has displeased her, and chagrin that her time with me was a burden that made her angry, rise up in me. "Is she always this harsh?" I ask Jessie.

She shrugs. "I'm new. She was pretty tough yesterday, though, with the other girls."

I feel pressure on my shoulder and turn to see Giselle hanging on me, her pale red hair twisted up in a knot. "We're about to see what the ballerina has to show us," she says.

My face feels hot. I sincerely regret not spending every waking hour at the academy working on my ballet skills. But there was the DVD trip, and the craziness of the fans wanting a rematch. Valentine's. And before that, all the trouble with Denham.

Excuses. All of them. I should have been dancing.

Now it was going to get me. That producer would be right. I'm not up for this.

I sincerely want to turn and leave, but Amara motions me out onstage. "Come on, Livia. And Giselle, back off her. We have to assemble a show here."

Blitz turns and fires an angry glare at Giselle. She blows him a kiss and turns away. "Come on, Mariah. Let's eat something."

Mariah doesn't appear to want to seem chummy with Giselle, but they both head back to the hall, followed by two girls in black, their assistants.

I walk out onstage. Blitz holds out his arms. I fold myself into him and he kisses my head. "How are you holding up, Princess?" he asks.

I can't even answer. I just want to stay right here, away from this pressure, the expectations, and the competition.

But sharp hand claps make me pull away.

It's Amara. "Okay, yes, we see who the love affair is. We still have to put on a dance show."

Devon saunters over. He's the director, dressed in jeans and a dark turtleneck much like the night I met him during the finale. He hugs an iPad to his chest, completing the picture that he looks like Steve Jobs, and frowns. "This star-crossed love worked great for the surprise appearance, but it's not going to sit well with the audience who wants a competition."

Blitz pulls me back against him. "I couldn't care less about your competition. And you know damn well all the fans want to see me with Livia."

"I don't know that," Devon says. "The rematch fury was pretty intense. It's my job to figure out how to spin this into a workable format."

"He's not going to be able to hide how he feels," Amara says. "He's not an actor."

Devon shakes his head. "I don't believe that either. We all saw him buying that diamond ring for nobody. That was good television." He walks in a circle around us. "We have to drive a wedge between the couple."

He tucks the iPad beneath his arm and holds out his arms in a V shape. "This allows a chance for the other girls. Only to snap shut," he claps his hands together, "when true love is threatened."

Amara steps forward. "All right. You work your drama. It's my job to create a dance number. She's not as strong as the others. We can work with that. Make him disappointed."

"No," Blitz says. "I will not have a negative thing to say about Livia's dancing."

"Honey, you won't have to," Amara says. "Her hesitation and inexperience are going to be evident." She looks out into the seats where a man sits behind a huge soundboard. "Ricky, give us a waltz."

After a few seconds of silence, the music begins.

"Just dance for a moment," Amara says. "Let's see where you are."

Blitz takes me in his arms. I try to forget everyone else and just follow him. I did it the night of the finale, tuned out the studio audience, the angry finalists, everything but him.

But it's harder this time. I'm not coming in for a surprise. There are expectations. Stakes. Blitz tries to turn us and I stumble, losing the rhythm.

He leans in close. "It's all right," he says softly in my ear. "We have nothing to prove. It's just a few months of our lives, five episodes, then we're done."

I settle in and let the music work its magic. I don't look at Amara as we pass, nor Devon. I follow Blitz's lead in the waltz, sweeping and turning with him, until finally, my nerves start to calm.

Chapter Seventeen

The next few days are a whirlwind. I work out with a dance coach, sometimes alone, sometimes with Blitz. Amara occasionally comes in to supervise.

Jessie follows me around, bringing me meals from the chef, filling my water bottle, and keeping Giselle at bay. For that, I am very grateful.

I have three dances to prepare. The first one will be on episode two, a waltz that expands on what Blitz and I improvised during the finale. Devon says we need to "show our love" since the other girls will have jazzier numbers.

For the "Classic Dance," we'll be doing a ballet-styled number with lots of lifts. My coach has me doing tons of abdominal crunches to make sure I have the core strength to hold the poses.

Even though I will probably be eliminated, we're also working on a number for the third live show, which is the "Sexy Dance." This will be a straight contemporary dance, which I'm not very well schooled on, but Amara is trying to make sure I can handle the positions if I get that far.

She hasn't prepared a dance for the final show yet. I'm assuming she will, or maybe we'll get to the eliminations before she plans that far ahead. I try not to think about the possibility that the home audience will vote me out right away due to my rather mediocre dance skills.

I don't feel like it will matter. In the end, Blitz and I will be together. After all, I'm the one who goes home with him every night. But it would be nice if the world was behind us.

The best part of the workday is when I get to practice with Blitz. For the past few months, we've had fun working out together and dancing on our own. But this is an entirely different level of togetherness. We have coaches, the choreographer, the costume designer, and Devon all watching our every move, preparing us to dance for millions of viewers.

Everything is heightened, each time our eyes meet, his hand on my back, every slide into a position where he lowers me down, his arm bracing me. The music is amazing, and when it all comes together the way it's supposed to, it's like magic.

I know he dances with the other girls too. I assume it feels different with them, more like work. But I don't know. I have to have faith.

Our evenings, of course, are mainly about crawling into bed and trying to sleep enough to feel ready to do it all again the next day.

Shelly was right. We have zero time to look at properties. She rides with us to the studio Friday morning to say that during our one day off on Sunday, she has lined up three places to view in a row.

Blitz and I are tempted to tell her just to pick one, but looking at them together is the right thing to do. The house we choose will be our home, the first place we can call ours. We should do this ourselves.

The property tours become the thing I look forward to. On Sunday morning, we linger in bed because we can. It's our first morning to snuggle in, not jumping up and preparing for another grueling day.

This room isn't even close to the size of the suite we had in San Antonio, so only half our stuff came to the hotel, the rest sent on to Blitz's camera-filled condo. Even so, we are surrounded by luggage and racks and boxes, so there isn't a lot of room to move around.

Because of the claustrophobic feel of the room, once we are up and about, we leave the hotel to have

DEANNA ROY

breakfast before meeting Shelly and the real estate agent who will show us the properties.

Blitz gave Duke the day off, so Blitz himself drives us around in the black SUV. I still don't have my driver's permit, and my little convertible was left behind in Texas. That will be something for another day. There's no way I could manage LA traffic anyway.

Blitz avoids anything trendy, settling on a little diner across the street from an old-school workout place called Buster's Gym. We have French toast and smoothies, watching the people come in and out of the facility, men and women who all look like they could seriously kick butt.

"I think that famous boxer used to work out there," Blitz says, stabbing a bite of egg. "The Cure. Cure McClure."

I catch a drip of syrup before it hits my chin. "I don't keep up with sports, but there's a big sign up there for Colt McClure."

"His son. He has like a billion MMA championships," Blitz says. "I think I was at some charity event with him last year." He shrugs and dives back into the decadent breakfast. This is one of the few days we can risk eating like this.

Shelly buzzes us that the agent is at the first place a little early if we want to get a jump start. We figure that's our cue to quit stuffing ourselves. We pay the check and head on over.

It's a beautiful February day. We wear sweaters but no jackets. The sun beams down. You can feel spring just around the corner, not that winter ever really took hold. It never does in Southern California.

Sometimes I think I could live here, but then I remember that Gabriella is in Texas, and I can't let her go. She will grow up, and I want to see what I can of her for as long as possible.

When Blitz pulls up to the first address, I feel shock. It's outrageous, stretching down the block, at least ten times the size of my parents' house back home.

"It's a lot," I say, peering out the window.

"Yeah, that's a big place," Blitz agrees.

We step out and shield our eyes from the sun as the chipper realtor comes over in her stilettos and beige suit.

"Don't you love it?" she asks, extending a hand. "I'm Tammy."

"Are they all this big?" I ask, shaking her cool, limp hand. Her hair looks like it just came out of one of the hair dryers you sit under at salons, big, blond, and airy.

"You will want space to entertain," Tammy says, clicking a button so that the tall iron gate slides open. "Let's take a look."

Blitz and I follow her uncertainly. Shelly pops out of her car and hurries to catch up.

"I tried to tell her you wouldn't be throwing big parties," Shelly says. Today she's in shorts and a pink tank top that matches her hair exactly.

Blitz takes my hand and we walk up the impressive drive. Shelly fusses with some keys and manages to open the door. "It has six bedrooms and five baths," she says. "Then another bedroom and bath in the pool house out back."

"I could live with a pool," Blitz says, pulling me close. He whispers in my ear, "I want to swim with you naked."

I squeeze his hand. The house is grand but the echoes of our footfalls sound depressing and empty. "We really need something furnished, don't we?" I ask. I can't imagine having time or energy to buy an entire house full of stuff.

"Oh, we can have it staged for you," Tammy says. "The designers will fill it however you like and pull it all when you leave."

I would argue at how expensive all that is, but then I remember those numbers on the contract. If mine were that big, I couldn't even imagine what Blitz's look like. I guess it doesn't matter.

"Are they all okay with a short lease?" Blitz asks.

"Three months is fine by them," Tammy says. "Although I'm guessing you might need six."

"Nope," Blitz says. "The finale airs in less than ninety days and we are out of here."

"All right," Tammy says. She stands in a formal room with glossy wood floors and windows that stretch along the entire back wall, looking over the pool. It's so Hollywood that I feel like people must film things here. Maybe that's why short leases are popular, and the staging of the furniture. It all starts to make sense.

"Doesn't feel very homelike," I say to Blitz.

"Agreed," he says. "What's next?"

"A condo about two miles from here," Tammy says. "I'll text you the address for your GPS."

And the morning wears on. The condo is on the fourth floor, and while there is an elevator, it's on the wrong side of the building. I can't imagine trudging up all those stairs after a long day of dancing.

The third place is another house, probably also used in filming. It seems vaguely familiar. It's not as large as the first one, though, and tucked in what feels like a normal neighborhood.

"Four bedrooms, three baths," Tammy says. "No pool, but there is a hot tub. Lots of living space."

We walk around. It's partly furnished already, the living and dining room fully set up, as well as bar stools set around a tall counter in the center of the kitchen. We'd only really need to outfit our bedroom.

"What do you think of this one?" Blitz asks.

I look around. The living space has a high ceiling, but the other rooms are cozy and close. Everything is beautiful, from the tile floors to the granite countertops.

"I like it," I say. "I think it's a good fit."

Blitz turns to Shelly. "Get us a bedroom suite, something traditional, and a king bed. We'll move in midweek."

Tammy claps her hands together. "Excellent. I have the lease agreement in my car."

"Let's do it." Blitz rubs his hands together. "A real place." He pulls me up against him and kisses my hair. "You were right. I'm glad we'll have somewhere to call home for a while."

"I'll cook you dinner every..." I hesitate, thinking of our exhaustion every night. "Hmm. Every Sunday."

"Sounds amazing," Blitz says. "I'll have to run over to my condo later to check on things. We're filming one of the dates there next week."

A chill passes through me. "Really? Who with?"

"Christy," he says. "She's been the most aloof and Devon thinks it will make us seem closer if I take her home."

"You mean to your condo," I say. "This is home."

"Yep, exactly that." He twists a piece of my hair. "This is not going to be easy, I know. Just trust me."

"I do," I say. *Just not them*, I think. Giselle especially will try to get him in a compromising position, just for ratings and drama.

Tammy brings the lease. Blitz signs all the paperwork and Shelly handles the transaction. Blitz and I walk around the house, holding hands.

"Our place," he says, turning me in a circle in the big empty master bedroom. "Can't wait to break in this room."

"You know, that living room ceiling is high enough to install an aerial silk," I say.

"It is." His grin is mischievous. "And I can think of a thousand things to do to you all strung up on it." He kisses my neck.

"Can you ask Shelly to have someone set one up? Will the ceiling hold it?"

He nuzzles beneath my hair a moment more before saying, "I'll let them figure out where the beams are. I'm just wondering if we can get everyone else to leave."

We hear Tammy's sharp heels coming down the hall. "Toodle-oo, Blitz, Livia!" she calls. "We're heading out! Keys are on the kitchen counter!"

"Perfect," Blitz says. We walk to the front as Tammy and Shelly head to their cars.

"That was quick," I say. "It's ours already?"

"It's ours already," Blitz says. "And I believe that sofa in there could use a little checking for comfort."

I laugh as he walks me backward into the living room. I have a feeling we'll be thoroughly exploring each and every room before it's over.

Chapter Eighteen

On Wednesday afternoon of that week, Blitz pops in my workout room at the studio. He's completely decked out in a suit, perfect hair, and shiny shoes.

"Whoa," I say, pausing my third set of ab crunches for the day. "You're all wardrobed up."

"Date night with Christy," he says. "It was on the schedule." He angles his head toward Jessie. "Ask her to get a copy of mine to go with yours. That way you'll know when I'm going to be gone."

My belly turns to cement. "Where are you filming?"

"Some restaurant and ballroom dance place. We're supposed to spontaneously perform. It's all extras. They bought out the place."

"Sounds fun. Isn't she the one you're taking to the condo?"

"Yep." He shoves his hands in his pockets. "You going to be okay tonight?"

I nod. "Sure. Is Duke going to take me to the hotel? Our furniture was supposed to be delivered today for move-in."

Blitz smacks his hand against the door frame. "Shoot. Today was supposed to be our first night!" He gives me a sad smile. "You wanna wait up for me there?"

At that, Jessie and the workout coach quietly exit the room. I don't blame them. They probably think I'm about to make some big scene.

But I won't.

"We're not checked out of the hotel yet, right? I'll ask Shelly to extend us one more night. We'll let tomorrow night be our first night there."

Blitz frowns. "I'm filming with Mariah tomorrow night."

I let out a breath. "How late will these go?"

"They need night shots. I think I'm walking along the Santa Monica pier with her. It will probably go super late. I don't even have rehearsal until after lunch either day."

I bite my lip, holding back tears. "Well, in that case, I guess I'll go ahead and move as planned.

Shelly's probably already got them packing our stuff and driving it over anyway."

He steps closer and kneels next to me on the mat. "I'll be there tonight, I promise. The part with Christy will go fast. We won't be at my condo for long."

I nod, resuming my sit-ups. I knew what I signed up for. Blitz has to put on a show.

"Hey," he says, pressing against my back so I can't go down into another sit-up. "I love you, remember? This is just work."

He gathers me against him. I hang on. He smells different, like hair products and aftershave, things he doesn't ordinarily wear. This helps. They've doctored him up for a role. He's not my Blitz. He's the version that belongs to the network.

I let him go. "I'll be the one sleeping in your new bed," I say.

"I can't wait to see you in it," he says. He stands up. "Jessie? You out there?"

Jessie steps timidly inside. "Yes?"

"What's on Livia's schedule for tomorrow morning?"

Jessie slides a messenger bag around her body, the one that carries all my things, cell phone, schedule, water, snacks. She unrolls a sheaf of papers. "Eight a.m. ballet workout with Caprice, then a dance rehearsal with Amara at ten. Wardrobe fitting at eleven."

"Tell Caprice she won't be at the rehearsal. We'll be here for Amara at ten."

Jessie nods. "I will."

"Tell them Blitz said it, not Livia."

Jessie nods again. "Got it."

Blitz turns back to me. "Bought us a lazy morning at the new place."

I squeeze his hand. "Thank you."

He presses another light kiss on my mouth and stands up. "I guess I'll go do this thing." He straightens his tie. "Christy is easygoing. This one will be fine."

"It's Giselle," we both say at the same time, and laugh.

"When is that lovely date?" I ask.

"Next week."

"And mine?"

"You are Monday." He heads to the door. "I got to choose the date, and they aren't allowed to leak it to you."

"Sounds like fun," I say.

"See you at home," he says.

"Bye, Blitz."

By the time the workout coach is back, I've resumed my ab crunches. I feel better, despite knowing Blitz will be out with Christy tonight. The cameras will be on their every move.

Still, I picture him kissing her, which I'm sure will be scripted or at least highly encouraged, and my stomach turns over.

This is going to be way harder than I thought.

~*´`*~

DUKE IS WITH BLITZ FOR THE EVENING, AND HE feeds me shots of the date with Christy while I supervise the team who is unpacking all our clothes.

I sit on the freshly made bed in the master bedroom, chain-eating chocolate cookies, simultaneously scrolling through the shots and showing the two women which drawers will be mine and which will go to Blitz.

As weird as it feels to have someone else arranging my stuff, I'm too tired to do anything more than sit and eat cookies, which were left by the real estate agent Tammy. A whole dozen of them and a bottle of wine. I might eat them all.

Shelly was here for a while, but I sent her home. Supposedly some grocery service will arrive within the hour to fill the fridge and pantry. She's mostly working with the chef's suggestions, but I had her add more chocolate chip cookies. My life has been missing cookies since I got to LA. Tammy was good to remind me of them.

"I think that's everything," one of the women says. They are both Hispanic and friendly, and just looking at them makes me miss Blitz. Has he called his mother since we've been here? I'm not sure. I should remind him.

"Thank you," I say. I'm too tired to even show them out, but thankfully, they leave on their own. Now that I don't have an audience, I flop back on the fluffy cotton duvet.

Another buzz from Duke.

Yes, he kissed her, but it was a silly peck. Devon's irritated.

A picture is attached, and I have to laugh. Blitz looks positively paternal as he leans in to Christy.

She looks incredibly lovely in an ice-white dress with little crystals along the neckline. They are at some restaurant on a dance floor and the lights make them look blue. It will be a good scene for the show.

I eat another cookie, hoping the grocery shopper brings some milk. Cookies and wine. Maybe that will do.

It will be hours before Blitz comes. They haven't even gone to the condo yet. I roll off the bed and head to the bathroom, looking around. There are towels now, all in various dusty pastels. A basket of shampoos and conditioners. Body wash. Razors. They've thought of everything.

For a moment, I flash to the bathroom at my parents' house back in San Antonio. My brother's Star Wars toothbrush. The Ivory soap and discount shampoo. A wave of homesickness passes through me.

I wonder if my parents will ever speak to me again, or if they are lost to me. What do they tell Andy about his sister? That she ran away? That I'm wicked and full of sin?

I can't even visit the places we used to go, so far away from Texas. I head back to the bed and my phone, pulling up Google Maps so I can zoom in on my dystopian park, bare ground and peeling equipment. Then down along the street to my house. The image shows Mom's old white minivan, the license plate blurred out.

The front is the same, the green door against the white clapboard. I look closer and I see on the porch a red wagon. It was mine as a child, moved with us from Houston for Andy to use. I can picture him in it. After Gabriella was born and my belly went back down, I was allowed to pull him in it to the park.

Another message from Duke.

Headed to the condo. Not long now.

I know Blitz doesn't even have his phone on him, but he might get it during the drive over.

And sure enough, a few minutes later, I get a message from him.

Shoot going okay. Sort of dull. The dance was fun. The extras at the restaurant were excited to be there.

I tap a quick message back.

House all set up. Waiting on groceries. Sprawled on the bed!

He responds to that.

Don't move a muscle. Can't wait to see you there.

I set down the phone. This will be okay. We will get through it. Of course timing would be bad. Our schedules are brutal.

I reach over for my bag. Jessie got me a printout of Blitz's schedule. Because of all the shooting he has to do, his dance rehearsals are shorter and less frequent now.

Tomorrow night he and Mariah will go to a night-club, also populated with extras. They won't do a showy ballroom dance like Christy, but something more casual and sexy. So the schedule says.

Mariah is the one who started all this mess. She filed the first lawsuit regarding the finale and got the other girls on board.

I roll back on the bed and stare at the ceiling. It's ten weeks. We can make it.

Chapter Nineteen

✻

Blitz gets in around two in the morning. We don't talk about the condo or his date. We have other things to do in our new home, and especially, the new bed.

When I wake up, I notice Duke sent me a couple pictures of Blitz and Christy sitting on his sofa, but I'm afraid to ask what happened, and what Devon and his cameras might have suggested happened. They'll do what they have to do to make the show interesting for viewers. I trust Blitz.

Even Mariah's date is no big deal. As I sit at home Thursday night, this time with a pint of strawberry ice cream, Duke reports that she's stiff and unnatural around Blitz, as if she's scared he'll be mad at her about the lawsuit. They only go to the club and take a walk on the pier after. Their date is done by midnight.

According to the schedule, my official date with Blitz is on Monday. The location is marked as secret. We haven't practiced any dancing for our date, so I assume ours will be different from the ones he did with Christy and Mariah.

When I arrive at the studio Monday, the workout coach puts me through only minimal exercises. Amara gives me some *pointe* work for the classic dance show number, and then I go straight to wardrobe to be prepped for shooting.

Jessie is waiting for me. There are three other women in the makeup room, one I remember from the finale.

"It's finally Livia's turn," the one says, and reminds me that her name is Cecilia. Her hair is still spiky, this time with blue tips. She turns to a tall stout woman with square glasses. "Will her outfit mess up her hair when she puts it on?"

The other woman shakes her head no. "It zips."

I wonder what they've picked out for me, and if that will give me a hint about where we're going. My nerves are prickly, and my stomach flits with butter-flies as if I didn't see Blitz every night.

This will be different. There will be cameras. People telling us where to go and what to do. These shoots aren't rehearsed, but Blitz said if something interesting happens, like if I trip and he catches me, they might ask us to do it again to get another angle.

Cecilia pats the chair and I walk over to sit on it. "Don't you worry, girl, we'll get you looking like a TV star."

I guess I'm supposed to be comforted by this. Apparently I don't look like one now? Does she say that to the other finalists?

I fold my hands in my lap. Cecilia unravels the braided bun. "Girl, you have so much hair," she says.

"What are you going to do with it?" I ask.

"I have to do what the stylist for the episode tells me," Cecilia says. "And I'm to make you look like a princess but prepare you for the elements."

"So I'll be outside?"

The square-glasses woman speaks up. "All the shoots are partially done outside. If the weather doesn't hold, we often have to make you up to look exactly like you did the day before and try again."

"Yikes," I say.

"It's going to be a beautiful night," Cecilia says in a singsong voice. "You are going to shine."

She starts rolling my hair into hot curlers. The other woman holds different color swatches next to my face. "Have Gigi tone down her skin, go blue," she says.

My voice is a squeak when I say, "Blue?"

Cecilia laughs. "Not like a Smurf. Just cool tones to your base color, not warm ones. To complement your dress and this black, black hair."

When all my hair is pinned up in rollers, the third girl approaches, angular with bangs cut in a dramatic straight line just above her eyes. She holds three skin-colored sticks and stripes them all on my cheek.

"Go blue, Gigi," Cecilia says.

Gigi rolls her eyes. "The skin wants what the skin wants."

"Well, Cameron wants blue."

"Cameron can stick to fabrics."

They continue to banter in this way as Gigi smooths more creams on my face. I'm turned away from the mirror, so I can't see what she's doing. She rolls a cart close and lifts the lid. It's chock full of colors, little circles in every hue imaginable. I see the blues and grimace.

"Not a pretty look," Gigi says. "It will cause wrinkles around the corners of your mouth."

I straighten my face.

"Close your eyes."

I try to relax as she continues to work. Without sight, the other senses take over. The smell of cosmetics and hairspray. The water running on the other side of the room. Hangers moving along a metal rack.

Then tugging on my hair. The rollers slide down my head. Nobody touches my face for a few moments, so I dare to open my eyes.

Gigi rummages around in her cart.

"What's the humidity today?" Cecilia asks.

"Forty," someone calls from deeper in the room.

"Forty," Cecilia breathes, as if this is a puzzle to solve.

Gigi leans in again. "Try not to blink or breathe," she says.

A mascara wand approaches my eyes. I try to keep them wide as she works. The square-glasses woman comes in again, Cameron, I guess Cecilia called her, this time with a pale blue dress. "Blitz called the color," she says.

I almost smile, but Gigi stops me with a stern "Don't move a muscle."

Finally, she steps away, and Cecilia takes over my hair in earnest. I feel her pinning and back-combing. Curls brush against my shoulders.

"She looks like Jasmine from *Aladdin*," Jessie says.

"Agreed," Cameron says. "It's what we were going for."

"She must have some Middle Eastern in her," Cecilia says. "Or maybe India."

Gigi studies me. "Yes. Her hair is so black."

"But she's pale as a ghost," Cameron says. "She would have more color."

I try not to squirm as they all assess me.

"It doesn't matter," Cecilia says. "Only that she looks more classically beautiful than the others. Those were our instructions."

Really? The world is a blur for a second as Cecilia whirls me around to the mirror. I feel like I did the night of the finale, needing to step down and get closer to this girl I see. The makeup is dramatic, and the sweep of my hair is broad, pinned almost like something from the forties, only to fall in a riot of curls down my shoulders and back.

It's me, just not a me I'm used to.

A girl I've never seen pops her head through the door. "Transport to the shoot location in ten minutes," she says.

"Get her dressed!" Cecilia says.

Cameron leads me deeper into the room, past the costume racks, to an area that closes off with a heavy curtain.

"Here are your underthings," Cameron says, setting a pair of pale blue ruffled boy shorts and a strapless bra on a cushioned bench. She hangs the dress on a hook.

I wait to see if she is going to leave, but she doesn't, so I take a deep breath and kick off my jazz shoes.

She taps her foot impatiently. "I need to make

sure it fits properly before I go," she says. "And I worry about the ruffles under the skirt."

I nod and take a deep breath, shucking off the dance top and workout capris, then the athletic bra. Finally, my panties.

Gah. Naked in front of a stranger.

Cameron is all business as she hands me the ruffled shorts.

I step into them. They slide on like silk, soft and smooth on the inside. The ruffles are mostly flat, although they pop out a little on my rear, making me a little curvier than I am naturally.

The bra looks difficult. The cups are shaped into a sweetheart, dipping down in the middle. The back is small with a single hook.

I press the front of it to me, and reach around to try and fasten it. After a couple misses, Cameron sighs and steps forward, fitting the hook in the eye.

She pulls the dress from the hanger and unzips it.

"Dive into it," Cameron says. "Arms overhead to protect your hair and makeup."

I lift my arms high and bend over. Cameron fits the dress around me and zips it up the back. It doesn't come up over my shoulders, but a band runs straight across the front and around.

The top is fitted, then as it hits the waist, it swings out. I do a quick turn, and the skirt flies up level with my hips.

"Now you see why the boy shorts," Cameron says. "Everyone wants you innocent, and he might twirl you."

She smooths the dress down to check the ruffles. "It's good," she says. "The fabric is heavy enough."

"What shoes am I wearing?"

"You have two pairs," Cameron says. She leads me back out to the main dressing room and picks up the boxes. "One is high heels, the other ballet flats. The stylist will tell you when to switch."

She opens the box and extracts the flats. I take them and slip them on my feet. They are blue and match the dress exactly. The stiletto heels in the other box are very bare, just a tiny strap across the toes and another at the back. They will be hard to dance in.

She passes the box to Jessie. Gigi tosses some of her makeup into a bag and waits. I guess she is also going with us. Cecilia, however, sits back on a chair. "Have fun!" she says. "You'll have a grand time. He's your boy, after all."

"Thank you," I say to her.

The girl from before pops back in. "Car is waiting!" She seems a little anxious.

My little entourage heads to the limo. I'm hoping Blitz will be inside, but when the door opens, only Devon is there, wearing his usual jeans and turtleneck. "We'll talk about what's going to happen on the way," he says. "Blitz is meeting us there. I want there to be a first look."

I slide onto the seat. Jessie comes in behind me, then Gigi with her makeup bags. It's time to do this.

Chapter Twenty

Devon goes over some of the basics of finding the active camera, how to sit and stand at proper angles for good shots, and explains that while they will record sound as they go, most likely I'll be going into a recording studio in a week or two to say again all the things I say tonight so they get good sound.

"It's hard to get good clean recordings at some of these places," he says, peering out the window.

He still hasn't said where we're going.

"You look beautiful," Jessie says.

"You do," Devon says. "Cecilia and Gigi did good work. Kendra will be pleased."

"Kendra?" I ask.

"The stylist," Devon says. "There are going to be a lot of people with you. It won't feel very private. Just do the best you can to focus on Blitz and not all the activity."

My stomach is a wreck. Lunch has passed and I didn't eat anything. I press my hand to my belly.

"I have fruit, nuts, and whole-grain crackers in the bag," Jessie says, attentive as always.

"Maybe a cracker," I tell her.

She passes me a couple, plus my water.

I try to eat them, but they taste like sawdust. I work harder to drink a little. Hydration is more critical than food.

The driver of the limo rolls down the glass between the front compartment and the back. "We are approaching," he says.

Devon rubs his hands together. "The success of this short season really hinges on this date," he says. "Livia, just let things flow between you and Blitz."

I pass the water back to Jessie. She looks so young in her blond ponytail and black T-shirt. "I've never been on a shoot before," she says.

"Just watch out for your girl," Devon says. "Make sure she has what she needs."

We roll to a stop in front of a gate. There are other limos here, and a few vans.

"Pull on up," Devon says. "You can't park on the street here, it's a right-of-way."

The driver nods and we turn up a drive.

At first I can't see where we're headed, then I

realize — it's a castle!

"What is this place?" I ask.

"The Stimson House," Devon says. "Beautiful atmospheric house. Lots of movies and shows have been shot here."

We pull up and stop, but Devon holds his hand out. "We need to get Blitz's location before you are seen."

The limo door opens, and a young man with a headset peers in. "Here's your set," he says, passing an earpiece and a small electronic box to Devon.

Devon clips the box on his belt and fits the earpiece to his head. "Big D on site. Can you hear me?"

After a moment, he says, "Location of Blitz."

Then "Move him to the dining room. We're going to go up."

He nods, as if the person he's listening to can see him. Then he looks at me. "Okay, all clear. We're heading in."

He leads the way out of the limo. I follow, then Jessie and Gigi.

The house is enormous and breathtaking. Large blocks of orange-red stone make up the exterior, sweeping up three stories, with a towering four-story round turret.

A wide stone staircase takes us up to a porch that could hold my parents' entire house. Devon looks around, nodding to himself, as if feeling assured that he chose the right place.

"What will happen here?" I ask.

"It will all unfold as it should," he says.

We go inside the heavy doors. Smooth round columns as big around as tree trunks separate the sections of the main floor. A wooden staircase goes up, light filtering in through stained glass windows inset in the wall.

"Let's go on up," Devon says.

I try to spot anyone else, but the main room is empty. Doors and halls branch off every direction. There is no telling where Blitz is in this maze.

We head upstairs. The rooms are amazing, wallpaper framed by ornate carved wood corners and baseboards.

"I'm going to deposit you ladies here," Devon says. "I need to check on the set." He takes off.

We look around our room. It's empty other than a couple chairs in one corner.

"You go ahead," Jessie says, and plops down on the polished hardwood floor.

I lower myself tentatively on the hard-backed chair.

"Let me check your lips," Gigi says. "Once we start shooting, you will only pretend to eat and drink. Don't actually do it."

"Okay," I say. I hope I can keep all these instructions straight.

She brushes more color on my mouth.

Then we wait.

And wait.

I'm tempted to get my phone from Jessie and text Blitz to see what is going on, but he probably doesn't have his phone either.

At least a half hour passes. Gigi checks me every so often and scolds me not to bite my lips.

I stand up and look out the window at the grounds of the castle. It's beautifully manicured, big green trees and boxed hedges, even in February.

Finally a woman comes in. "Livia, ready?"

I take a deep breath. It's time.

When I get out on the landing, there is barely room to walk. Devon is there, cameras, lights, a whole crew of people.

"I want B roll of her feet, the skirt, her back," Devon says. He turns to me. "Livia, we're going to have you go up and down the stairs a few times."

"Okay," I say.

"Hand on the rail, lightly," Devon says. "Go down gracefully. Like a ballerina."

I nod and touch my fingers to the wood banister and start to go down. I'm anxious to see if Blitz is below, but once I'm halfway, the only thing I see are more cameras, more lights, more crew.

"All right, Livia, back to the top," Devon says.

We repeat this a few times.

"All right," Devon says. "Let's move on."

I'm back at the top of the stairs. There is a sharp turn in them near the bottom, so I can't see around the bend until I make it most of the way down.

"All on the face," Devon says. "Long, medium, and tight." Then to me, "Livia, come on down. This time, he'll be waiting."

My chest relaxes out of its tightness just knowing I get to see him. I touch my hair, then place my fingers on the banister as before. Everything feels heightened, the light beaming in through the stained glass, the gloss of the wood, the shimmer in the moiré pattern of the wallpaper.

I take each step carefully, with intention, as if I'm a ballerina coming out onstage. I can sense everyone's interest in what I'm doing, the cameras rolling, crew members sliding their rigs along a smooth track.

When I make the turn, I see him. My breath catches. He wears a white shirt and a black vest over dress pants. He's perfect. I'm as swept away as the first time I saw him.

His eyes dance as they light on me. My focus is only on him as he holds out his hand to me. Now I feel like I'm floating.

The cameras slide farther back as I take the last few stairs. At his feet are a blanket, a picnic basket, wine glasses, and cheese on a china plate.

"You look beautiful," he says, "like a princess."

I feel my cheeks heat up. "Is that why you chose a castle for our date?" I ask.

I hear the quiet sighs of the crew. They are thrilled with our exchange. I have the sense that this moment is both real and unreal, scripted and spontaneous, planned yet still ours.

I reach him, and he takes my hand to kiss my fingers as he always does. "I could think of no place more suitable."

I look around. "It's very fancy."

He pulls my hand to his chest. "You want to look around?"

I sense that this move has been suggested to him, but I nod and play the part. He leads me to a fireplace, then to a dining room, and we exclaim about the details of the woodworking, the ceilings, the intricacies of the space.

Soon we're back at the blanket and the wine and cheese. I kneel down and he sits with me.

This time, Devon interrupts.

"Let's place them for the lights," he says.

Blitz grins at me. "They let us go longer than I thought they would."

I look around. There are so many people. A dozen at least. Gigi rushes in and powders my face and shifts one side of my hair behind my shoulder.

An older woman in a bright tunic and tights

comes forward.

"Blitz, you should be here," she says, tapping the corner of the blanket. "And Livia, I want you more here." The center.

Devon also comes forward. "See that camera there?" He points at one dead ahead. "That's our primary angle. Make sure you don't block each other from that one." He points up. "Jerry, get that shadow off Blitz."

A photographer snaps a few stills as we rearrange.

"Now that you've got the position," Devon says, "let's take it back to the dining room, walk in, and take it straightaway."

I nod. Blitz helps me up and we head back to the dining room.

Now the spontaneity is truly gone. I remember a scene with Blitz and one of the early girls on his sofa, kissing. Did they do this then? I lean in. "Will they be there telling us how to have sex?"

Blitz chokes back a laugh and starts coughing. "They record every word we say," he whispers. "Take it easy."

"You didn't answer the question!" I hiss.

He shakes his head. "That part is just for us." Then he pauses. "Unless that turns you on."

"No!" I squeak. We've made it to the dining room.

"Roll that footage for continuity," Devon says. "Let's get him in place."

The woman stares at a screen partially hidden by a hood. "Switch places, guys," she says.

She's right. I was on the left before. We move back into position.

"Close enough," Devon says. "Let's move."

We walk back to the picnic, this time settling in the predetermined spots.

But as soon as we're down, Devon stops us again.

"Kendra," he says.

The woman in the tunic hurries forward. She adjusts my dress, shifts my ankles, and frowns when she sees my shoes. "She's in the flats!" she says.

Devon shrugs. "We already have too much footage of her feet," he says. "Leave it."

Kendra is seriously miffed, but she adjusts my hair, Blitz's vest, and shifts the plate a little closer to us.

"And rolling," Devon says.

Blitz reaches for my hand and kisses my fingers again.

"It's becoming a habit," I say.

"Because you're delectable."

It's such a Blitz thing to say, on his show, not to me normally, that I can't help it, but burst out laughing.

"What?" Blitz says.

"It's me now!" I say. "Or is there a real me and a show me?"

Blitz nods, his expression thoughtful. "You're right. I was acting. I've been acting, on this show, with all those girls. But I don't have to be that way with you."

I bite my lip, then stop, remembering Gigi's admonishment. It's hard to fight my awareness of the cameras, imagining how they'll zoom in on my face, then shift to our joined hands. I can picture the people watching, breath held, waiting for me to respond to this confession.

It's us, but not us. We're here, but not here. It's intoxicating. I feel so important, like what I say and do matters.

"You know what is best about us?" I ask him.

"What?" he asks.

"When we're together, it's not just about us. It's about all the things we love."

"Like your wheelchair ballerinas," he says.

My expression falters for a moment. I can feel it. Gabriella. I miss her already.

"We'll be back to them soon," he says. "And you're right." He pauses, and I get the impression that it's so they can cut the scene here if they want to leave out the part about the ballerinas. "I love our life."

"Together," I say.

Blitz lifts one of the glasses of wine and hands it to me. Then he takes the other and clinks mine. "Together."

Chapter Twenty-One

We film on the picnic blanket for over an hour, until my legs ache from the position and my back starts to complain. Jessie comes forward with water and pain relievers, then Gigi fixes my lipstick.

"Sunset is coming," Devon says. "Let's reset in the side yard."

The crew begins moving, and Blitz and I carefully extricate ourselves from the blanket.

"This date is going to go way longer than our real first date," I say, relieved to know the cameras aren't on us at this moment.

"They always do," Blitz says, helping me off the blanket.

Kendra approaches with the shoe box. "You're switching to these now," she says firmly.

I sit on a bench and put on the stiletto heels. Blitz passes the flats back to Kendra.

"What do you think of how it all works?" Blitz asks me.

"It's interesting. I keep imagining people watching me, though. It's very surreal."

Blitz nods and takes my hand as I stand up in the heels. "You get used to that feeling."

"I keep second-guessing everything I say."

"Just be you," he says. "If you try to imagine how they will cut and splice every sentence, you'll go crazy."

I hadn't even thought of that. They could rearrange parts, take them out of context. My face blazes hot. Would they do that? They could make me look crazy, or stupid, or angry. They could take one yes and switch it with a later no.

"Do you trust these people?" I ask as we follow the last of the stragglers out to the yard.

"As much as you can trust anyone in Hollywood," Blitz says. "But I never forget they forced me here."

Devon motions us over to a grassy area. Another blanket is spread here.

"It's the date of picnics," I say, not really looking forward to sitting on the ground again.

This time, we're arranged from the beginning. Blitz leans against a tree and I curl into him. I like this, and immediately go to lay my head on his shoulder.

"The hair!" Kendra says, leaping forward to smooth it down.

"This is tedious," I say.

"Welcome to television," Blitz says.

Eventually we get to another little period where they leave us alone and let us talk without interruption. Like Gigi said, we don't actually eat or drink anything from the set. It's just there to look pretty.

We break for a brief dinner, Shelly showing up with meals from Blitz's chef, light salads with nuts and berries.

"We need some walking, some kissing," Devon says next. "Now that it's dark, we'll be hand-lighting."

I set down my salad, and Gigi rushes up to me to fix my makeup and lipstick. "I'm giving you some hardcore stain so you don't smear," she says. "But expect that every kiss, we'll have to fix you before we can move forward."

"Okay," I say.

We head back outside. The path is narrow through the heavy foliage.

"Follow the lights," Devon says. "Places!"

Blitz and I stand at the end of the walkway, holding hands. We follow a string of lighted globes, although the real brightness comes from big lamps strapped to the trees overhead.

As we walk, I start to hear the sound of music. We pass a large leafy bush and there stands a lone violinist in rolled-up sleeves, giving us a charming smile as he plays a waltz.

"I believe he is playing our song," Blitz says.

"I think every waltz is our song," I say, then think, that's a promo moment.

I'm right, because just as Blitz takes my hand to lead me in a few steps, we're stopped and asked to repeat those lines several times in a row.

"I'm going to see a commercial with this on it, aren't I?" I ask Blitz.

"I hope so," he says.

Finally, we're released to dance along the path. The lights whirl into a blur as Blitz turns me on the narrow sidewalk. It's not easy to navigate the way in flimsy heels on concrete, but Blitz keeps the steps simple. Mostly we try to smile at each other, which isn't hard. The setup is truly lovely.

"I think it's time for kissing," Blitz says.

"About time," I say.

He makes the steps smaller and slower. The music has faded as the violinist stops following. But when Blitz leans in, we're still dancing, turning. I have an inspiration and pick up the side of my dress, letting it sweep out as we turn, faces together, lips brushing lightly.

I can see the image onscreen, the blue dress lifted

out, the soft grass, the lighted path.

I have to believe the audience will root for us.

Chapter Twenty-Two

W hen we arrive back at the studio the next day, Devon stops by the workout room to congratulate me on some amazing moments.

"It was gorgeous," he says. "The castle, your dress, the way you and Blitz were together. TV magic!"

I press my forehead down, easing into a stretch. "I'm glad it went well."

"Spectacular!" he says. "Now we just have to get you ready for the live shows. The host, Barry Winston, will be by at some point to chat with you, then you'll do some quick spots with him, sometimes dressed and made up, sometimes more natural in here during practice." Devon looks around the practice room. "The other ones have more light. We might switch you and the other girls around."

"I understand," I say.

"You'll do great," he says and heads for the door. "Loved the castle work. Really truly did."

I'm glad he's happy about how the date went. And I'm not worried about the next two dances. My *pointe* is looking really good and ballerinas are always special. It's something none of the other finalists are trained in.

It's the sexy dance that scares me. I'm not like that. I don't prance around. I don't know contemporary style. I feel my confidence from last night starting to wane.

Plus, I know tonight is Giselle's date. Blitz is feeling some fatigue. I can see it in his eyes. The girls only have one late night. Blitz has to do them all.

I think the others see it too, because they cancel my rehearsal with Blitz in the afternoon. He goes on to wardrobe for the Giselle date. Since this leaves an empty space for me too, I decide to go see him.

When I arrive at his dressing room door, I hesitate. I've never gone inside. Then I berate myself for that. Out of everyone in this cast and crew, I have the most right to walk in there. I'm the one who sleeps beside him every night!

But still, it feels like trespassing, as if this version of Blitz doesn't quite belong to me.

I knock on the door.

Hannah answers it, and I'm shocked to see her. I

thought Blitz wasn't speaking to his manager. She's smug and put together in a pale yellow suit.

"Can I help you, Livia?" she asks.

"They canceled our dance practice," I say. "I thought I'd hang out with Blitz while he's in wardrobe."

"That's not a good idea," she says. "They're doing some candid filming."

"I can hide with the crew," I say. "I saw last night how it works."

Hannah's face is set. "Not going to happen. Now run along."

Oh my God. My face flames. She's treating me like a little girl! When Blitz is mine!

"No, thank you." I push her aside and head into the dressing room.

I am completely unprepared for what I see.

Giselle is in there, wearing only a pair of panties. Her arms are draped over her chest for modesty. A camera is aimed at her and a crew member holds a panel so that it lights up her bare skin.

And she is sitting on Blitz's lap!

I feel faint, absolutely faint.

Blitz's back is to me, but Giselle can see me perfectly. She gets this smirk on her face, but keeps her arms where they need to be for the shot. "Oh, look who has arrived."

Blitz sees me, and there is no shock there. Just

tiredness and resolve. "Up to their old tricks," he says. "Television drama."

I immediately understand what he's doing. If he talks like that, they can't use the shot, because it's not right for the show. It's talking about the show.

I could follow his lead. Talk about the producers or the director or something that isn't usable.

Or I could take that bitch down.

I take a deep breath, remind myself who I am, and calmly step forward as one of the cameras eagerly turns to me.

"Giselle, put some clothes on," I say. I pick up a nearby towel and toss it to her. "Or don't bother. Everybody's already seen you naked. It's not even interesting anymore."

She does what I think she will, which is to automatically reach for the towel before it hits her. Her boobs fly free, making it a nude shot, and no longer usable.

Blitz immediately realizes what I've done and bites his lip to keep from smiling.

I head over and take his hand, pulling him out of the chair, which forces Giselle off his lap. "You seem tired. Let's grab something to eat before you have to do any more shooting."

"Works for me," he says.

He's dressed at least, already in a shiny button-down shirt and pants. So I lead him out of the room and into the hall, knowing the cameras won't follow. I roll my eyes at Hannah as we pass. Might as well be the kid she thinks I am.

"Did you know they were going to do that?" I ask.

"Only about five minutes before they did it," he says. We head to the viewing room, where Jessie and Shelly usually wait with our lunches if they aren't with us.

"You figured it out when they canceled the rehearsal?"

"Yeah, that's their MO when they are going to spring something on me," he says. "Plus there were too many cameras in the dressing room for random footage of getting ready for a date."

I want to ask if she came in naked or stripped for him, but I'm guessing I'll find out when it airs. Uggh. This job.

We head into the viewing room. There's a smattering of people. A couple of other dancers, eating salads, and several of the assistants, including ours. One of the girls in black, probably Giselle's girl, pops up when she sees Blitz and takes off for the door.

"I guess you were supposed to have taken longer with her," I say. We sit at one of the tables and Shelly and Jessie unpack our coolers.

Blitz rubs his eyes. "I really wasn't up for those antics when I have to spend all evening with her," he says.

"I wish I could come with you and help out," I say.

Blitz laughs. "This sounds so ridiculous, right? My girlfriend coming with me on a date."

"Like some terrible made-for-TV drama," I say with a grin. "Oh...wait."

Blitz smiles and I sense him relaxing a little.

This is hard on both of us.

I lean in to whisper in his ear. "I'll be waiting for you when you are done with her," I say.

He closes his eyes a minute, then he says, "If I look at all like I'm anticipating something wonderful in this part of the episode, it will be you."

We eat close together, our shoulders touching, until Shelly lets him know it's time for him to go.

We are going to get through this.

Chapter Twenty-Three

From what I hear, Giselle's date is a bust. She keeps trying to get him to kiss her, push her against the wall, look like they are having sex. But Blitz is having none of it.

Duke's texts are hilarious.

She-cat's in heat!

Blitz just ordered her raw steak and called her a cougar. Oh, she is mad!

I'm pleased it was horrible, but also know that those antics will get a lot of airplay. It's just too Tweetable.

The next week's shooting is so much easier. No dates. No late nights. Just dancing, set, wardrobe. There are a few interviews in the dressing room like Devon said, questions about my dancing history and what I will be doing with Blitz. I meet the announcer

Barry and he laughs about how I charged on the stage for the finale, leaving him speechless for the first time in his life.

I hear rumors that there are arguments between the other girls caught on camera, but I'm left out of it, other than the accidental one with Giselle. I hope they don't try to manufacture something on the live show. I don't know how I will handle it.

It feels strange not being able to see what we've done so far. I want to know how the date episode looks, how my practice footage is working, if I should adjust. Devon assures me I'm doing fine and that the editing is going well.

The first hint I get about what will go into the episodes is when I'm sent to the recording booth to say some of the lines from the castle date.

A sound engineer shows me around. There's a big screen showing a still of me on the staircase in the castle, and a microphone and headset next to a transcript printed out of what I said.

I finger it all, fascinated. "So I have to say it again?"

"Yes, we'll practice it so it matches your mouth."

He points to the door. Devon has come in and pauses in front of the screen.

"When you came down the stairs," Devon says, "what you said was perfect and how you said it was perfect. Unfortunately, you took a big echoing step on that wood staircase, and we lost a word."

The engineer plays the moment with the original sound. I watch eagerly as the footage shows me walking down the steps. It cuts to Blitz, and he says, "You look beautiful, like a princess."

Then I say my line. "Is that why you chose a castle for our date?"

And I hear it. I take a step down on the word "castle" and it disappears in the CLUNK sound of my shoe.

"All we have to do is have you record the line again. It might take a few tries to make it match," he says. "But we'll get it."

I glance at the transcript. "Do I have to redo everything from that night?" I ask.

"Oh, no," he says. "That would be too expensive. There's only five lines, I think. This one, one on the floor when a microphone buzzed, and a few outside where we just didn't pick you up."

I nod and look at the page. We practice the castle line a few times, and the engineer explains how I'll hear three audible beeps with flashes, then the flash with a silent beep is when I start talking.

I mess up the first couple of tries and talk too soon or too late, but then I get it. We have the new lines recorded again quickly.

Devon stands up as I pull my headset off. "Good

work, Livia. It's nice to have the prerecorded show about ready to go. It will air in a couple weeks and then we'll be ready for the live ones."

He pats my shoulder and takes off. I'm about to follow him when I notice another sheet below mine. I shift the top page aside and see some lines that Christy will have to rerecord. I quickly read them.

"I just want us to have a chance, Blitz."

"Tell me you're not really in love with her."

"She can't feel as passionate about you as I do."

My stomach sinks. Were there others?

The third page is full of Blitz lines, all from the castle. Nothing for Giselle or Mariah.

I glance up at the screen again. The last scene I recorded was during the waltz, when we thought no one could hear us. I had whispered, "I love you."

I sure hope I'm not going to look too stupid on the show. I keep telling myself it won't matter. In the end, Blitz will walk away with me, no matter what the television voters decide.

But I do still have pride. And I am still a little afraid.

Chapter Twenty-Four

Even though we're not filming, we still have plenty to do to prepare for the upcoming live shows. The series premiere with episode one is a week away, and this will set the tone for what the TV viewers will think as they learn they are now in control of the winner of *Dance Blitz*. Voting will begin on live episode two.

I didn't realize there would be a red carpet premiere viewing until one day during ballet rehearsal, Jessie pops in to say I'm expected in wardrobe in five. This isn't on my schedule.

I slip out of my toe shoes and head down the hall. Cameron and Kendra are there with a rack of glittery gowns.

"What are those for?" I ask. None of them look easy to dance in.

"Two designers are vying to show off their dresses at the premiere," Cameron says. "These are on loan, so each of you girls have to choose one and send the rest back."

I approach the row of dresses in a half-dozen colors. "So there will be cameras on us?"

Cameron and Kendra exchange a look. They have no idea that I was banned from TV and social media for years. Only in the past few months have I been able to connect with the world, and Blitz surely hasn't done any premieres since I've known him.

"I've decided to let Blitz's look be determined by yours," Kendra says. "I assume you two will go together, no matter what the producers say." She sorts through the rack.

"The producers don't want us going together?" I feel lost and confused.

"Of course not," Kendra says. "It spoils the illusion that this is actually a competition."

The urge to snatch my phone and look at the other season premieres is intense. "Who did Blitz go with to the others?"

"Stag," Kendra says. "Of course. It was in his contract. They must have known not to try it this time around."

I walk up to the dresses. "We're just in this to finish out his obligations. It doesn't matter how it goes in the end."

Another glance between the women. I know Kendra went on all the dates as the stylist, but I had insider information on that with Duke. Does anyone here actually believe the contest is for real?

I've been fairly isolated from the other finalists, but now I wonder why. Are they plotting things I don't know about? A tremor of fear runs through me. Is there anything they can actually do to hurt us?

Kendra turns to the rack and pulls off an aqua-blue dress. "I like this one."

Cameron considers it. "Do you think we're over-doing the blue?"

"Possibly," Kendra says. "But the public's memory is short. Even with just four contestants, we want to make sure they always know her from Mariah."

This makes me want to scream. Mariah and I look nothing alike.

Kendra sees my expression and says, "Livia, there will definitely be hard-core fans who will know your every expression, but for a lot of the casual viewers the two dark-haired ones are going to blend together."

She holds the dress up to me. "I think it's good to keep her in blue and the others out of it, like the Virgin Mary." She laughs and I burn inside again.

"Go try it on," Cameron says. "And don't damage it. It's all on loan."

I take the hanger from her and head to the

curtained section. The dress is heavy, beaded from top to bottom, shifting in color from almost white at the top to a medium blue at the bottom. All the beads are white, which lightens the overall tone of the dress. It's very beautiful, and very simple, just slender straps on top with a square neck. When I put it on, it spills on the ground in the back like a wedding train. It's a couple inches too long in the front as well.

I pick up the skirt as I walk back out to show the others.

I'm more than a little stunned to see Mariah and Christy in the room.

"More blue," Mariah says simply.

"It's the color Blitz loves on her," Christy says in a singsong voice. The two of them laugh like it's some big joke.

I ignore them and turn to Cameron. "It's too long," I say.

"Nothing some killer heels won't solve," she says. She tugs on the bodice, waist, and back. "It's a good fit. Not a standout dress, but very pretty."

"What do you have for me?" Mariah asks.

The four women go over to a different rack. I assume I must be done. I spot Jessie in the corner and she gives me a sympathetic smile.

When I'm back in my ballet outfit, I carry the dress out. Cameron and Kendra are still sorting through dresses with Mariah and Christy, so I just hang the dress up and leave. I can see I'm not their priority.

I tell myself again that it doesn't matter.

When Jessie and I get in the hall, the assistant choreographer runs up to say Blitz is ready to rehearse our number for the second live show, the one where I do a ballet. I'm completely relieved to be able to see him after the stress of the wardrobe room. I send Jessie back to the workout studio to collect my toe shoes.

The stage is mostly empty, although our prop for that dance is partially constructed. It's a tall, pale blue fake ice sculpture of a goddess, robes flowing, her hair blowing wildly out. It matches our dance, which depicts the ice goddess thawing with the arrival of a man.

Blitz is talking to Amara, who is showing him a deep gentlemanly bow. He tries it, and she adjusts him over and over again. I sit on the floor to tie on my toe shoes. Amara sees me and gestures for a girl holding a flat stiff pancake tutu to approach.

When I stand up, she lowers the tutu so I can step inside it. She seats it properly on my hips, then hooks the closure in the back.

I've never worn a pancake tutu, only flowing ones, and as soon as I lower my arms, my wrists smack into the stiff netting. I jerk them back up.

"That's why we're practicing with it early," Amara says. "They take getting used to for both of you. Blitz will have to get accustomed to dealing with the distance he'll need to keep to avoid smashing it."

Interesting they are doing this. In a classic tutu like this, we'll have to stay at arm's length, like the most traditional ballet.

"I guess we won't be making out onstage," I tell him.

He smiles. "I can get around any obstacle." To prove it, he leans over and presses a kiss on my mouth.

"All right, from the top," Amara says. "It's going to feel very different with the costume. Blitz, don't forget the bow."

As we run through the dance, the spotters moving forward with each lift since we might run into trouble with the tutu, I realize how stilted and formal it feels. I wonder if I'm being sabotaged. The dance is pretty, and I think the viewers will like it. But we're not talking about choosing a ballet partner. This is about making a commitment with someone.

And with this dance and this getup, we're going to look like we barely know each other.

Chapter Twenty-Five

With most of the prerecorded film spots done, and lots of rehearsal clips ready to go, the schedule slows down. We get Saturdays as well as Sundays off. Blitz and I decide to seek out the instructor Bex told us about so we can do more work with the aerial silks.

The new instructor is male, and he really helps Blitz get a feel for how acrobatic the silks can be. We develop a few simple moves as a couple that are new, including an impressive drop where I appear to fall off the silks and Blitz catches me. It's more startling than pretty, something you'd see at a circus rather than in the context of dance.

Despite Blitz and I spending far more time apart than we had in San Antonio, I feel we're doing better than before. We're more aware of our time together and don't take it for granted. Blitz takes me to the beach, and Rodeo Drive. Sometimes we rent a random car and work hard not to be seen.

Other times, we take a selfie with the location obvious, and hang around for the inevitable crowd to form, asking for autographs and taking pictures.

Blitz and I don't talk about it out loud, but I get the sense he's trying to ensure that when the live voting starts, there is plenty of support for the two of us, and the other girls won't have a chance. I guess some might call it sneaky or underhanded, but honestly, he just wants the world to be on board with what he's already decided.

Me.

I'm crazy anxious when the team arrives at our house the morning of the premiere to start the prep. It's eight hours until we step onto the red carpet, and everyone is already complaining about not having enough time.

Blitz and I are separated so I can be waxed, polished, manicured, and coiffed. The makeup girl is new. This team isn't the *Dance Blitz* crew. Shelly helps supervise and coordinate since I don't have a manager. I wish I had a way to get Jessie here, but I only ever see her on the set.

The blue crystal dress is delivered and I'm fitted into it six times with different undergarments. There's talk about my hips being too bony, my boobs too flat. Some want more butt, others want more cleavage. I become an object rather than a person. They try push-up bras, stick-on bras, no bra. Then thong underwear, ruffly underwear, and some spandex thing that makes me feel stuck in a chute.

Apparently I have no say in any of it. My hair is curled into elaborate spirals. My makeup is the most dramatic I've ever seen it. Bright coral lipstick, winged eyeliner. My cheekbones have never been so prominent.

Almost no one talks directly to me. I'm like a mannequin or a doll. I long for Blitz. Jessie. Cecilia. Even Hannah would be an improvement. As soon as I think that, I know I've gone around a bend.

Blitz is whisked away well before I'm done. He comes in to kiss me and say he'll see me at the premiere. I want to ask if he has to go see the other finalists, but I'm afraid of the answer, so I don't.

The process is tedious, and embarrassing, having total strangers applying wax to places I don't understand why they are messing with. My gown is full length with a train. I'm not exactly going to be flashing my bikini area.

But finally, as mid-afternoon comes around, they pronounce me ready.

I get my shoes last, deadly stilettos so high as to feel like I'm *en pointe*. The heels are tiny, like a spit for the barbecue. They are silver and gleam with sparkle, an exact match for my toes and fingers.

I stumble twice trying to cross the living room, and the woman in charge relents and carefully rolls my dress and fastens it with pins. I'm allowed to slip off the shoes and put on pretty silver ballet flats for the ride only.

The chef sends up a salad with thin crackers and a vitamin drink to get me through the evening. I suck it down greedily, not having eaten since this crew arrived, but halfway through the water, one of the women shakes her head and takes it from me. "Go pee out what you can," she says. "Or we'll have to put the spandex on you."

I hurry for the bathroom, very much not thrilled when one of the women follows me in to ensure the safety of the dress while I pee. When I wash my hands, she holds a towel in front of my belly to avoid splashing it.

"Why is this such a big deal?" I ask.

"This dress is on loan," she says. "You cannot damage it."

"If I damage it, I'll just buy it." Money has started hitting my own account.

"One hundred and twenty thousand dollars?" she says.

Um, okay. Never mind. I look down at the dress. It is worth more than my parents' *house*.

I realize for the first time I have zero jewelry to wear. I wonder if that will be noticed, and why none was borrowed if they were going to go to the trouble to get a dress on loan.

We walk back out to the living room. Most of the crew has packed up. Out front, a limo waits.

Now that all the prep is done, I feel very much alone. I have no one to talk to, and I imagine having to arrive in the limo by myself, facing the cameras and fans and reporters without anyone directing me. Panic flits through my body. What if Blitz is already there posing with Mariah or Christy or Giselle? Do I walk up and do the same?

A driver in a black suit and hat stands by the door. I nod at him as he opens it. I feel like I'm driving to my doom. This might as well be a hearse.

But when I lean in, I see him.

Blitz.

I let out a small cry and lunge for him. "You're here!"

He wraps his arms around me, careful not to disturb my makeup or the dress. "Of course I am," he says. "You didn't think I was going to send you out there by yourself, did you?"

I settle beside him on the seat. "I wasn't sure."

The woman who had directed the crew of people comes inside the limo. Blitz nods at her. "Hey, Steena," he says. "I figured you'd be doing Giselle."

"Giselle brought her own staff for this event," Steena says with a sniff. "No telling how she'll turn out."

Blitz turns to me. "You look devastatingly beautiful. Your picture is going to be everywhere tomorrow."

"Our picture," I say. I realize he's holding a box in his lap. "What is that?"

"For you," he says. "They were going to get something on loan, but I decided I wanted to buy you something special."

I look around. There is no camera crew here. He's not doing this for effect, for an audience. It's just us.

He passes me the box.

I open it and suck in a breath. It's a necklace, all diamonds, like little leaves in a perfect circle.

"I got it approved for your dress," he says. "Kendra said it was fine."

I can't stop looking at it. "Blitz, this is crazy."

"We should indulge in a thing or two before we settle down to ordinary life," he says. "We probably won't have much occasion to dress like this once the show is over."

He lifts the necklace from the box and unclasps it. "May I?"

I nod and turn away from him.

His fingers slide across my skin and the diamonds lay cool and heavy against my collarbone. After he fastens it, he presses a kiss into the back of my neck. "Like it?"

"It's breathtaking," I say, touching it with my fingertips.

"Just like the ballerina who wears it."

I turn back to him. "I'm so nervous," I confess. "But I'm better now that you're here."

He tucks my arm inside his elbow. "This is great fun. The limo will pull up, we'll get out, and there will be outrageous cheering, a lot like the DVD signing."

"Will girls show their boobs?"

He laughs. "I doubt it. We'll be in front of a big sign advertising the show, and they'll want pictures of us together. Then probably apart." He squeezes my arm. "That's normal, even with married couples. They like to have individual shots for the fashion people."

"Okay," I say. "Then what?"

"We'll walk down a ways, and there will be a reporter who interviews us. Again, together and possibly also separate."

"What about the other girls?"

"Usually they spread us out," he says. "But due to the competition and the drama, you never know."

"We're making our approach," Steena says.

"Where are Devon and the rest?" I ask.

"Already there," Blitz says. "We'll be the last to arrive. The big finale."

I take a deep breath.

Steena passes me the stilettos and I slip the ballet flats off and put the other shoes on. Then she comes behind me to release the dress from the pins. "Be careful in this," she says. Her voice is kinder now. Maybe she was anxious earlier too. Maybe seeing how Blitz treats me changed her mind about who I was.

She scoots down the long seat to the very front near the driver so she isn't accidentally caught by the cameras as they snap us coming out.

"I'll get out first," Blitz says. "Then I'll turn and reach for you."

"Got it," I say. Another deep breath.

"This is easy," Blitz says. "I actually have fun at these things."

The limo rolls to a stop. I hear cheers as the door swings open. I can see bodyguards on either side of the carpet.

Then Duke peers in. He's pretty cleaned up in a black suit. "Don't fall on your face, bro," he says.

Blitz shakes his head. "Don't trip me."

Duke steps aside and Blitz exits the car. The roar of the crowd is tremendous and flashes pop like crazy. He turns for me. "Ready?" he mouths.

I step carefully across the floor and bend down to emerge from the car. When I appear, the cameras go crazy all over again.

Holy cow, I'm here.

Chapter Twenty-Six

The walk up the red carpet takes a while. Every time we take a step, someone else calls out, "Blitz, Livia, look this way!" and we stop and smile again.

We're separated, like Blitz said we would be. I try to look natural and smile, but I'm sure I appear to be a lost child in the images. I've had more photos taken of me in the past five minutes than in my entire nineteen years.

When we get to the first reporter, Blitz says a few words and then everyone asks if we will kiss for the camera. Blitz is more than happy to oblige, dipping me low as cheers and whoops carry on in the crowd.

I feel more than a little dizzy as he lifts me back up. This whole experience is heady. I can see why people would get addicted to it.

Finally we're led into the theater itself. The lights are all up over the crowd. It isn't as large as I thought it would be, only maybe twice the size of a typical movie theater. Devon is in front of the screen, talking into a microphone.

"And here is our star, Blitz Craven, with the lovely Livia Mays."

I hesitate a second, then remember that I have a stage name now. We wave to the crowd. Devon gestures as if he wants Blitz to come up, but Blitz shakes his head and we move toward the front row. For the first time, I see the other finalists.

Giselle is ridiculously beautiful in a deep black gown, her pale red hair in an elegant chignon offset to one side. Mariah is queenly, her hair an elaborate braided updo, in a tawny gold sequined dress. Christy looks lovely in white again, almost bridal, her blond hair flowing in gentle waves across her shoulders.

Our chairs are marked. I'm to sit next to Christy, and Blitz is on my other side.

We settle in. Devon goes on a little longer about the history of *Dance Blitz*, making jokes. Barry Winston, the host of the show, comes out for a moment, saying a few disparaging remarks about Blitz, sending the crowd into titters more than once.

Blitz handles this all fine, draping his arm around me and crossing one ankle over his thigh. He seems relaxed, like this is his element.

Finally, they clear the microphone stand and the opening credits to *Dance Blitz* come on. There's a cheer in the back, and I realize there must be fans here as well as cast members. I wonder how they get tickets. I wish I could have gotten my friend Mindy here somehow. She would have loved this.

When the show begins, I'm completely captivated, as if the characters onscreen are other people. The host recaps the last season that led to the three finalists. We see brief clips of some of their dance numbers, and at least one kiss with each girl.

I find myself gripping the armrest during this, and Giselle notices and smirks. I let go and try to appear more relaxed.

Then we see Blitz walking across the room where he always deliberates on the girls before he chooses. He looks at Giselle's image, then Christy's, then Mariah's.

Then he opens a drawer and extracts a fourth matching frame. When he turns it around, it's a photo of me.

He sets it closest to him.

The host is back. He says, "This season is extra special. In this episode, we'll introduce you to Livia Mays, the new girl who surprised millions of viewers by storming onto the live finale last December."

They play a clip of me coming onstage.

"Blitz will go on four dates, one with each girl, as

we prepare for four live episodes. And this time, *you* get to choose who is eliminated each week."

He quickly runs through how the show will work. Four elimination episodes, all with live voting. At the end of episodes three and four, a girl will be sent home.

My stomach flutters.

The rest of the show goes through our dates. Blitz dances with Christy and gives her a chaste peck at his condo. The pier with Mariah, and Duke was right, she seems stiff and unsure.

Then me, at the castle, coming down the steps, and dancing on the path. They don't use any of the footage of us sitting on the ground, and I apologize to my unhappy legs that they went through all that pain and suffering for nothing.

The host comes out. "We know Livia has the advantage going into the live shows, but there is one wild card in the batch. The girl who has always gotten under Blitz's skin. Giselle Andreas."

There's a flash of a nearly naked Giselle on Blitz's lap in his dressing room. Then a montage of things that must be old, as Blitz's hair is a little different and so is Giselle's. Them kissing. Blitz pressing her against his Jaguar, his hand going up her skirt.

Now I'm having to force myself to stay calm. My heart is beating so hard that it hurts. I've never seen most of these moments, even though I watched both seasons. They must be outtakes they didn't use before.

The two of them roll in sand at the beach, her untying her bikini top and flinging it away. Blitz hides her and waves the cameras away.

Barry comes back onscreen, the images shrinking to a small rectangle behind him. "It will be up to you who gets the final dance with Blitz Craven." He glances back at an image of Blitz and Giselle gazing into each other's eyes.

God, it looks like they were meant to be together, the way the clips are done. I'm just one of the other three. It's completely opposite of real life.

Blitz reaches for my hand and squeezes it.

By the time the lights come back up, I can barely breathe. They want Giselle to win! They definitely want her to stay until the end.

We all stand, and people come up to Giselle and kiss her cheek. Mariah and Christy look over at me uncertainly. I know I must be pale. My face feels numb.

Blitz is easygoing and congenial, greeting people, shaking hands. I'm mute and shocked, like a statue beside him. But he sticks by me.

The time ticks on, never-ending, horrible. Giselle pops over, leaning on Blitz and kissing his cheek long enough for many pictures to be taken. I clutch his hand on the opposite side, unable to say or do anything about it.

Finally, at last, the gathering starts to break up. There's talk of drinks, an after-party.

I can't do it. I just can't. The lights are so bright. The noise so loud. I feel like an explosion has just gone off and my ears are ringing, and I'm barely able to recognize what used to be familiar.

When we make it to the limo, Blitz is all smiles, bouncing with energy. I don't know how he hasn't noticed my distress. I don't know how to explain to him why this is so horrible for me. I can't explain it to myself.

He asks me what I'm up for, if I want to attend the after-party, and finally registers my expression, the stiffness in my arms and neck.

"Livia, hey, what's wrong?" He pulls me close.

I can't answer, my face going to his chest, the fancy hairdo coming undone, me coming undone. It's like there's a vise around my lungs, and I can't take in enough air to say a word.

He instructs the driver to take us home and holds me close. I feel the energy and excitement drain out of him, and I wonder, am I right for him after all?

Chapter Twenty-Seven

I don't feel much better even after sleeping. I don't want to get up.

Blitz isn't in bed with me. I peer at the tops of the bedroom curtains and realize the sun is blazing. We have the day off from rehearsal, thankfully, or I would clearly be late.

I check the clock. After ten.

My hair is a horrible disaster of pins and hairspray. This must be what a hangover is like, except I didn't drink anything. I feel like the comic book drawings of someone recovering from a bender.

I manage to tame my hair into a crazy ponytail and pad into the living room. Blitz is on the sofa, surrounded by a laptop, iPad, and the episode schedule, while also talking on the phone. He winks when he sees me.

"Those are some really great numbers," Blitz says. "What will it take to show me results before it airs?"

His face is serious. "I don't get that. When did I get cut out of this loop?" His expression gets darker and darker.

"I'll talk to Devon about it." Then he abruptly hangs up the phone and throws it on a cushion.

"Hey, Princess," he says, shoving aside the laptop. "Come sit with me."

I head over and curl up on his lap. My feet are freezing on the tile.

Blitz is completely put together, showered, dressed, looking much more formal than usual in a button-down shirt, vest, and black jeans.

"Everything okay?" I ask.

"Oh, I just wanted to see how the live results would be tallied. Normally I can twist someone's arm to release the data early. It is *my* show."

I breathe in the smell of him. Pine woods. Shampoo. I'm surprised he's so presentable on our day off.

"You going somewhere?" I ask.

"There's a publicity thing this afternoon," he says. "Sort of spontaneous. Optional. I'm going. The other girls will be there. Signing stuff. Nothing official."

I close my eyes. I don't want to see them again. I don't want to do this at all. I feel all my muscles contracting.

"This is a hard gig," he says. "I'm not asking you to go. But I need to be there."

I nod. I want to tell myself to shower, to pull on some clothes. Call in a makeup person. Be bold. Get in Giselle's face. Do this.

But I can't make myself. I slide away from Blitz and fold up in a ball against the arm of the sofa.

"What's happening to you is really natural, Livia," he says. His voice is soothing. "You want to escape all this. I get it. Tons of the contestants went through it. When you see yourself up there, it really hits home how vulnerable you are." He scoots close to me again so we're touching. His hand smooths my hair away from my forehead.

"You want to know a little reality TV secret?" His face is so close that I feel his breath on my cheek.

"Okay," I say.

"On a lot of these shows, whether it's singing or dancing or eating worms or just being bitchy housewives, most of the cast doesn't leave the show over straight eliminations or judges or being voted off the island."

He pauses. I can't summon the energy to respond to this, so I just listen.

"They quit. They walk out. The show saves face by showing footage that leads viewers to think it was their singing or bad attitude or whatever. But often, it's just nerves."

He kisses my hair just over my ear. The warmth of him is comforting.

"Normally you would have gone through a vetting process. Auditions, interviews, screen tests. Your ability to hold up under pressure would have already been tested, and even if you made it through that on my show, any sign that you were cracking would have meant I got a blue card on you during early filming."

"Blue card?"

"The first elimination round is big. I have to get rid of several girls at once to thin the field of contestants. If anyone on the crew, from the assistants to the cameramen to the wardrobe people, felt someone was caving in, they would tell their supervisor. Devon would get it, and issue me a blue card, which meant I had to eliminate them."

"Would I have gotten a blue card after last night?"

Blitz wraps his arms around me. "I think you did fine. I know you felt like you were frozen and overwhelmed, but you didn't show it. Have you looked at any of the commentary on the premiere?"

I shake my head.

He reaches over for his phone. "Let's see. I'll read you some."

I shift and snuggle up against him. I know he won't read me anything I can't handle.

"Okay, here we go. 'Livia kept her cool while

Giselle played the fool. Let's vote that ho off on the first episode.'"

I smile. The public doesn't mince words.

"And another one. 'Livia was like a calm queen among the reality TV attention whores, including Blitz. She can do better.'"

This makes me laugh. "Who is better than you?"

"Oh, you'll get plenty of suggestions. In fact, I think there were at least five marriage proposals on Twitter last night. Duke was forwarding those."

"I like Duke."

"Yeah, he's all right."

"I didn't trust him after the Twitter thing. I thought he was involved."

Blitz shuts off his phone. "I admit to having my concerns too. But it wouldn't really be any benefit to him to tank my career. He'd be out of a job."

"Where is this signing thing?"

"At a bar one of the producers owns."

"Not the mean red-faced one."

"No, the quiet one, Drake Addler."

"His name sounds familiar. Not just as a producer. But something before."

Blitz plays with a loose curl that is falling down my cheek. "He was a child actor. Did a show where he was a Dennis the Menace type kid living with a rich family."

"I remember that!" I used to watch reruns of the

show, in the time before my father took the television away.

"He was smart with his money. Now he produces other shows."

"So we like him?"

"He'll be there. You can judge for yourself." Then, realizing what he's said, "If you want to go."

I realize I have no help. No wardrobe. No makeup. "When does it start?"

He checks his watch. "About three hours."

"Is there any way I can get Cecilia here?"

"I'll call Shelly."

"Okay. I'll go shower."

Blitz smiles. "That's my princess."

I uncurl myself from the sofa. I'm better. I see how things are. And Giselle is good for us. She draws all the attention and takes all the negative hits. Of course Devon would capitalize on that.

They are making Giselle into a cliché, the bad girl, the whore. And there's one thing that tends to be true in Hollywood.

The bad girl never wins.

Chapter Twenty-Eight

The intensity in the studio starts reaching a fever pitch as we enter the week of the first live elimination show.

Rehearsals are brutal, especially for Blitz, who practices with all four of us and ususally has to go on talk shows each evening.

When we more or less have the waltz and the ballet down, Amara leaves the supervision of work for the sexy dance to her assistant, who is a hundred times nicer. She has me wear very revealing body suits and work on getting comfortable with another male dancer standing in, his face pressing close to mine, his hands skimming me.

I know this show is important. If I get that far, the sexy show is the last vote, the one that will determine who wins on the final episode. It's intended to spike the ratings.

We do other exercises I find strange but stirring, watching and mimicking sexy movie scenes, and reading aloud passages from romance novels and doing spontaneous dances to match. I think I'm pretty open to things, but some of them make me seriously blush.

By the time I get home each night from these exercises, I'm more than a little hot for Blitz. Because of his publicity gigs, I always get home before him, and I've tackled him before he can even get something to eat.

He doesn't complain.

The morning of the first live show feels a lot like the finale did, only I'm there for the entire process, not just the show itself. It airs at eight Eastern, so five our time, and preparations begin at six in the morning.

The stage has been transformed since that last live show. Huge video screens flank the two sides. The upper stage, which has been roped off for days, has a new false floor with lights running beneath it.

The bottom stage is lined with neon and is where we perform most of the dances, although some of them involve both sections. We have final rehearsals in costume now that both stages are integrated. The lights and sound will also be tested with us rather than our stand-ins.

My first run-through is with the ballroom dance coach, as they are working not to overtax Blitz. Once Devon has made adjustments to my position as well as the chorus dancers, Blitz comes out.

My heart hammers as he walks up in his dance costume. Our waltz is meant to continue my princess theme from the castle date. I have a deep blue dress with an enormous skirt that billows when I turn. He wears a soldier-inspired outfit with epaulets on the shoulders and frog fasteners down the front, his legs in heavy dark blue tights.

"Places!" Devon shouts. Cameras shift into their locations. They are practicing their roles too. I realize now how much chaos my appearance at the finale created for the well-rehearsed production.

We are bathed in darkness as Barry comes out to introduce our number. On the video screens, images from our castle date tell the story of who we are. A phone number and texting key shows up, with the reminder to download the app or go online.

I wonder if Mindy will get to watch and use all her votes for me. I make a promise to myself to call her house from an unknown number and try to get through. Maybe I can get Jessie to do it, and once she's on the line, switch to me.

The lights come up and the music begins. Blitz

smiles down at me, and I take courage in knowing that of all the dances, ours matters most to him. Everything else is just theatrics.

We begin our path across the stage, which is set to look like a ballroom. Extras in fancy gowns wait on the edges as if entranced by our solo dance. The video screens are still images of windows in the walls of a castle.

We dance and spin, flawless, graceful. My love for him surges. We are doing this. We are getting through it.

The extras come out to fill the upper stage, so Blitz and I move to the lower one to finish out the dance. We twirl and he lifts me momentarily, then we turn out and back. The final notes arrive and we whirl into our final position and hold.

All the lights come up. "Very nice. Blitz and Livia, walk to extreme stage left, where you'll do your interview with Barry. Once you hit the mark, you can go. Dancers, we need to make a few more adjustments."

Blitz and I hold hands as we head to the far edge of the stage, where Barry will put us in the spotlight for a post-dance interview while the set is changed.

Once we're in position, Barry tells us, "I'll say, 'How did that feel?' and you'll say, 'We feel great, Barry,'" and if something happened I'll bring it up, but otherwise we'll hang here for about ninety seconds of chitchat, then you'll exit that way." Barry points behind us.

"Got it," Blitz says.

Jessie walks up with a bottle of water and Shelly comes to put a towel around Blitz's neck.

"You guys change out with wardrobe," Amara says. "We're done with you. Livia, you'll need to be in makeup in thirty. Blitz, we'll do the next number as soon as you're changed."

I nod. Blitz squeezes my hand, then takes off for his dressing room. I give the water back to Jessie and tell her I'm going to watch rehearsal and to come get me when it's time for makeup.

Then I hurry down the steps of the stage and sneak into the audience seating. I sit down in the highest, darkest corner.

The number is run through again with the dance coach and a trainer standing in for me and Blitz. The trainer doesn't know it perfectly, but the coach more or less leads her through all the positions.

The chorus dancers in their big gowns are so beautiful, led by male dancers in outfits that mimic Blitz's but in muted tones. Astounding. I can't believe I'll be dancing in it. It will be so exciting for everyone at Dreamcatcher to see back home.

I wonder if my parents know. If they'll look.

My throat feels thick.

The lights go up onstage and the extras for the

ballroom scene exit. There's several minutes where spots go on and off and the video screens flash random footage, blank out, and come back. Barry moves to various places on the upper and extreme side stages while they play with lights and colors.

Then the crew removes the pedestals and flowers for the waltz and bring out an Eiffel Tower and several pillars of fake stone. A Paris scene. I wonder whose it is.

I don't have long to wait. Like with my rehearsal, Mariah comes out with the dance coach. She is in a long glittery black gown. Her hair is in a lovely tight chignon covered with black net.

I watch the clips that precede her dance. A few are the same from the first episode, and others are different. Blitz kisses her on the Santa Monica pier, the Ferris wheel behind them, and my stomach twists a little. He has no choice. I know this. But I feel sick just the same.

Their dance has more technical difficulty than mine, with lifts and spins while she's held suspended by the coach. A twinge of jealousy flutters through me that I'm not as good as her. But she's probably danced all her life. Her poise and training is evident. Every movement, arch, and position is perfect.

When the lights come up, she gets back in place and waits. Blitz comes out again, still tugging on his cuffs. He wears a black and white tuxedo for this number, and my heart squeezes at how handsome he looks.

They greet each other and wait for the darkness to go down. Barry runs through his part again, then the clips, and the cameras move.

Blitz is different from the coach in subtle ways. His movements are not as precise or technically perfect, but he has a smoldering quality that makes the dance more emotional. He tugs at you, making you wish it were you he was dancing with.

The lifts are good, and the quality is definitely there. But Mariah is not quite as on with Blitz, as if his style doesn't really lead her to be the best she can be. I wish the voting audience could see this. It's so clear that they are not perfect partners if you see her with another dancer back to back.

I wonder if I'm allowed to vote.

A door opens from above, creating a rectangle of light from the hall. It's Jessie. I hurry to the hall to head to makeup, wishing I could see all the numbers. Just watching this one has definitely bolstered my confidence.

Chapter Twenty-Nine

T he last half hour before we go live is incredibly intense. Everybody runs from place to place with wardrobe emergencies or lost shoes or wondering where the heck the hat boxes went.

I'm dressed and made up and calm. I go on first, so I am in and out before any of the other finalists. Now I hole up in my dressing room, supremely glad I get this small space of my own.

Jessie sits nervously on a chair near the door, checking her phone every ten seconds. "This is so exciting!" she says. "I'm so worried I'm going to screw up!"

"You'll do fine," I say, finding comfort in calming her. I haven't seen Blitz since we passed in the halls a few hours ago, him pulling off a necktie on what looked like a forties getup.

There's a knock at my door. Jessie opens it to a huge arrangement of flowers that hides the person coming in.

"Oh!" Jessie says, propping the door wide. "Look at this!"

I stand up. The arrangement is at least three feet wide, an explosion of roses and white lilies.

"Who is it from?" I ask.

The flowers move to the side and I see it's Blitz!

Jessie takes the flowers from him and sets them on the counter, then quickly exits the room.

"You ready for this?" he asks.

"Honestly, this isn't nearly as bad as the last time I came," I say. "I know what's going to happen."

"True," he says. He gathers me close. "Gigi will kill me if I wreck your makeup, but I just wanted to see you before it all starts."

"I'll be here when it all ends."

He touches my shoulder, my cheek, my hair. "You look breathtakingly lovely. You'll captivate every viewer out there."

"Let's hope they agree when they vote," I say.

He laughs. "You've been turned to the TV dark side," he says. He presses a light kiss on my forehead. "See you onstage. I love you."

"I love you too."

He's headed for the door when I see a strange red light in the corner. As Jessie comes back in, talking excitedly about the flowers and the people outside, I step closer to it.

It's coming from an ornate mirror hanging on the side wall of the dressing room. Jessie stops talking as I peer closer at it. It winks out.

There's another knock and another delivery of flowers.

"This one's from Bennett Claremont," Jessie says.

But I'm still looking at the small oval mirror. I lift the edge to take it off the wall, but it won't budge. I pull harder, and it finally swings open.

There's a camera inside.

"Oh!" Jessie says. "Was it recording you?"

I glance around, wondering how many times I've changed in here, what footage it would have. I close it back up.

"There are cameras everywhere," I say. "It's in the contract."

"That's so creepy," Jessie says. "They should tell you where they are."

"They told us we'd sometimes be filmed in the dressing rooms. I just didn't think about it being run without a person in here too." I turn to the main mirror, wondering if there's something behind it as well. "From now on, when I change, I think I'll have you hold something up."

"Agreed," Jessie says. "Wow, that's invasive."

"Welcome to reality TV," I say.

_*´`*_

As we approach the time for the show to start, the TV screen in the top corner of my dressing room pops on and the live feed of the stage is piped in. Currently it glows blue from the *Dance Blitz* logo and the neon lights along the floor. In the corner beyond the stage, I can see a hint of the studio audience entering and taking their seats.

My stomach flutters again.

After a few minutes, the TV flashes and switches to the actual broadcast, a commercial and lead-in with the *Dance Blitz* theme.

I watch as the lights go up onstage and Barry walks out. He's just started talking when a girl in all black comes in the room. "Five minutes," she says.

I nod. Barry describes how to vote, and the website and app download flash on the screen. He explains that viewers have forty votes that can be divided any way they like but they must be cast within two hours of the end of the show. Then he talks about each of the girls, and little interview clips and dance rehearsal footage are shown.

I'm deeply engrossed, when the door opens again. "Places," a girl says.

I stand up and Jessie follows me into the hall.

Kendra approaches and checks my dress and makeup and hair. "Break a leg," she says.

The dance coach rounds the corner and waves at me. "Remember to relax into that last turn," he says.

"Got it."

He pats me on the shoulder as he passes by.

We enter the backstage area, completely black except for low red lights and the occasional rectangle of a viewing screen with a hood surround. When we get close, I see Barry out onstage, looking up at the video screen. They must still be running the montage.

I feel a hand enclose mine and turn to see Blitz. His eyes shine as he looks down at me. "Love you," he mouths.

"Love you too," I whisper.

The lights go back on Barry, drawing our attention back to the stage. He walks to one side, saying, "We'll be right back after this message."

This is our cue to carefully go out into the darkness and wait for our dance to start. The chorus dancers start to fill in around us.

Then we're back live. Barry talks about me a little, and the screens show the castle date footage just like in practice. I sense the cameras moving into position.

Then Barry is back. "For our first number of the night, the couple you've been waiting to see again in person, the princess who stormed the castle to save her prince, Livia Mays, with our dance bachelor Blitz Craven."

I'm not quite ready for the applause and feel a little startled. But as the music starts up, I'm able to tune it out.

The number runs exactly as planned, no stumbles, no big mistakes. I'm a little nervous, not quite as at ease as during the rehearsals, but I don't think it's anything too noticeable.

We take a bow and head to the side stage to meet Barry. My stomach flutters. A live interview. I almost trip on the hem of my dress, but Blitz squeezes my hand and keeps me steady.

"That was truly lovely," Barry says, grinning broadly. His dark gray suit gleams as much as his dark hair. "How did it feel?"

"Amazing," Blitz says. "I'm so happy to be back onstage with Livia." He gazes down on me with utter fondness.

I lean into him automatically. "I would never want to dance with anyone else," I say.

"Oh, ho!" Barry says. "That's a lot to live up to, Blitz. Is the Texas ballerina trying to tie you down?"

"She already has, Barry," Blitz says.

Barry looks out to the audience. "If you agree that Livia is the girl for Blitz, remember to cast your vote."

We exit the stage and are plunged into the semi-darkness of backstage.

"I must run, my love," Blitz says with a quick kiss on my hair. "See you after the show."

He heads to wardrobe to prepare for Mariah's number. I hesitate a moment, watching the chaos of the set change, the new chorus dancers, and the crew shifting everyone around.

Mariah passes me.

"Good luck," I say. "Your Paris number is beautiful."

She looks back a moment, not sure what to say, it seems, then nods and moves on. The pattern begins again, commercial break and montage. I realize she'll have to go out alone and wait for Blitz. I was lucky to be the first one, so he was dressed and ready for me. He'll be increasingly harried as the show goes on.

Not that it will matter. He's a professional. But it is only his second live show.

I lift my skirt to avoid tripping and head out into the hall. Only when I'm back in my dressing room, now full of flowers from all the producers and one from the girls at Dreamcatcher, do I relax and watch the rest of the broadcast.

Chapter Thirty

W e don't get to know the results of the show. Nobody does. Some independent technology company tallies and verifies the results.

Because there is a "last dance" for the girl who gets eliminated at the end of the next live show, we all practice a quiet, simple number with Blitz in addition to our "classic number" that we will be judged by.

I try to reason with Kendra and Amara about the pancake tutu for our ballet. It's in the way, I explain, and it means Blitz and I can't embrace, not even in the post-interview.

But they are stubborn about this. I wonder what is going on.

More footage is taken of us practicing. Giselle is often seen roaming the halls in nothing but a tiny satin robe, looking for cameras.

I tape a piece of paper over the oval mirror so the camera in my dressing room can't get any footage I don't want. I spotted a couple clips in the montages when we rewatched the show that looked a little hazy, like they were behind two-way mirrors in the other girls' rooms. I didn't see anything that would have been from the camera in mine.

While there was a definite emphasis on Giselle in the opening show, the live show was extremely even-handed. We all had the same type of footage, inter-views, dance rehearsals, and date footage.

But somebody up top wasn't happy with the low-conflict nature of the show. So a session where all four girls get together to be chatty is scheduled. It will be held at a restaurant where we will all eat lunch together.

The luncheon is a fiasco. I'm not asked to say anything ahead of time, but the other girls pick fights that are obviously scripted. Mariah accuses Giselle of sleeping with Blitz just to get an in. Christy points out that Blitz doesn't have a say anymore in who wins, so why would anybody sleep with him?

I wonder who gave them memos and left me out, or maybe they just talk to each other and not me.

For the most part, I stay quiet and wait between takes for the prop people to remove food from our plates so it looks like we're actually eating.

But the next time the cameras roll, Giselle turns

on me. "So the goody-two-shoes ballerina thinks she's got a lock on Blitz."

My face burns, and I pray it isn't as red as it feels.

Mariah and Christy try to tell Giselle to back off, but she goes full drama queen, standing up and throwing her napkin on the table. "He was in love with ME!" she says, her eyes tearing up. "We have a connection." She points her finger at all the other girls. "He quit sleeping with everybody to be with only me."

She smooths the sides of her skintight coral dress. "Let me tell you all," she says in a hiss, "that nobody gets Blitz Craven off like I do." She leans in to me. "And no fresh-faced, naive teenager from podunk Texas can turn him on like I do."

And that's when I lose it. And I say something I shouldn't. And I know they will air it, because that's what reality TV shows do.

I sit up tall and say, in my most prim and naive voice, "He didn't mention that when he was tying me up in aerial silks and making me come while suspended from a four-poster bed."

Well, that shuts her up.

The assistant director, who is supervising for Devon, bites his hand in excitement over my outburst.

Giselle looks at him. "I think you got what you were looking for," she says, and walks out.

I guess that was who was sending scripted ideas to the other girls.

Mariah and Christy look at me sympathetically. "That is going to go so viral," Christy says. "Maybe even more than Blitz's terrible Tweet about Giselle."

I sit quietly and wait until both camera operators are packing their stuff before I say, "He can't stand her, you know. He didn't mean to Tweet that thing, but he was tired enough of her to say what he did."

Jessie appears and hands me my bag. "Let's get out of here," she says. Even at sixteen, she knows when I should quit.

I don't want to ride in the studio limo, where Giselle is probably sitting and stewing. Or maybe it was all faked. I don't know. I feel sick about the whole thing.

I'm supposed to go back for a workout with my trainer, but for the first time since I joined the *Dance Blitz* cast, I go full diva.

"Jessie, go grab that taxi," I say, pointing to a yellow cab dropping an elderly woman off at a shop a few doors down. She takes off to nab it.

When I get in, I tell the driver my home address and give Jessie cash to cover going back to the studio.

"I'm not feeling well enough to work out today," I say.

Jessie nods her approval. "You need a break."

I send a text to Blitz to let him know what I've

done, blabbing about our aerial silk sex. I don't think he'll get it for a while since he's flying back from a morning show in Seattle, but he surprises me by writing back immediately.

The pressure gets to all of us. I think it's hilarious. Can I do it again?

This makes me smile. Just three more shows and we're out.

Chapter Thirty-One

❧❦❧

The second live show is similar to the first. There is a different feel to it, though, since we know someone has been eliminated, and her dance tonight will be for nothing, since the votes won't count after she's gone.

Someone will be going home.

I almost hope it's me at this point. After the hidden camera, and the luncheon gaffe, I'm pretty sure I'm not cut out for this game.

But my *pointe* looks good. I've improved faster than I would have at home, motivated by the demands of the show.

Our set is very simple, just a few white pillars. My costume is extremely stiff, not just the pancake tutu, but the bodice. It doesn't really move with me, but around me. I wonder if regular ballerinas have outfits like this and have to manage. I could have used pointers from a professional, but it's too late now.

I dread the moment when my lunch comment goes live. Nobody's seen the clips. No one's talked about it. The public doesn't know, since only staff and paid extras were in the cafe.

I feel sick to my stomach as I head through the backstage to do my dance with Blitz. I'm later in the lineup this time, third instead of first, so I'll have to go out alone and wait for him and his costume change.

I've kept my screen off in my room, hoping I miss seeing myself be vulgar, as my dad would call it. God, I hope now that they are avoiding the show. Have people at church seen it and asked how such a quiet sweet girl got here?

I feel like I can never talk to them again after this.

Blitz says I was baited to say it. That Giselle was probably instructed to get me to say something trampy to increase the raunch level of the show, because that was the expectation of the viewers. He'd done way worse.

But he is a man, and the fact is, he doesn't feel the stab of being called a slut. Even Giselle seems to want that image and lets it roll right off her. But I don't.

The show goes to commercial and I head out onstage. My dance starts as a solo with me on the ground, lost and alone until Blitz comes along. I like the music very much, and I think the story of the dance is beautiful and true.

But I'm full of anxiety about the clip. I pray they don't play it while I'm out there waiting. They didn't show anything during rehearsal, as one of the monitors wasn't working, causing a tech panic.

I can really only listen, as my head is down. There's a little clip from last week's dance, I know that by the music. And Blitz's princess line from our castle date.

Then Blitz saying, "You'll captivate every viewer out there."

I have to glance up at that. It's the footage from the dressing room. It looks really good for being behind that two-way mirror. But it still makes me burn. At least they can't use that camera anymore. It's covered now.

The screen shifts to the dance background, and I drop my head again, relieved they didn't run the lunch footage.

The music begins. I start the dance, unfolding like a flower around the difficult tutu. I go up on *pointe*, slowly, carefully, and the audience claps.

Then Blitz is there, taking my hand, and I turn uncertainly to him.

We dance gently, then with growing certainty,

until I go into one heck of a dizzying spin. The studio audience is roaring with approval now.

Then our dramatic end pose, and freeze.

"Perfect," Blitz whispers.

We head over to Barry. If the show goes on the way the first one did, a chit chat interview then on to the next contestant, I'm in the clear. Maybe they decided my quote was too bad for television. This makes me smile.

"Somebody looks happy about that performance!" Barry says.

"She was amazing, wasn't she?" Blitz asks the crowd. They scream and cheer in response. "Are you voting yet?" More noise.

"Do you feel things are going well between you two?" Barry asks me.

"Perfectly," I say. "He's an amazing partner."

"Well, you two looked great," Barry says.

We exit to the back. I let out a long breath. No mention of the clip. Now there is just Giselle's dance and the elimination. Then someone will slow dance as a farewell.

Rather than making us all change, which would be very hard for Giselle, since her dance and the elimina-tion are back to back, we are to stay in our costumes for this one. I wait backstage with Jessie. Mariah and Christy, who have already danced, are also in the wings.

Giselle passes, wearing a red and black dress that looks like a rose. They must be doing a tango, which would make sense for them. That was always their dance.

Jessie comes up beside me. "You were great!" she whispers.

I nod and watch the stage. Our order isn't as much about strategy on voting as Blitz's outfits and how much change needs to happen. He rushes back by in black satin pants and a matching shirt. He carries a rose.

They are good. I wouldn't call their dance extraordinary. But clearly it is a crowd pleaser, as the audience hoots and cheers for every dramatic turn. When it ends, Giselle and Blitz head over to Barry.

A girl motions to me, and I follow Christy and Mariah to the edge of the stage. We don't go out until the commercial.

Barry announces the break and we three girls walk forward.

Blitz takes a long pull of water as he heads to center stage. I don't know how he does so many dances in a row. He must run on pure adrenaline.

The crew rapidly removes the tango set.

The four girls line up together and hold hands like we were instructed during practice. I'm between Christy and Mariah.

It's strange and intimate, holding their hands. I'm just glad I'm not near Giselle.

Blitz passes his water to a crew member and they rush off.

The lights come back up. Barry says, "And now it's time for one of these lovely ladies to go home."

The crowd makes a collective "awwww" sound.

"Your votes have been tallied from last week. First we are going to announce the two girls who led the numbers." He opens an envelope. "These girls will definitely be back next week. Mariah and Giselle."

My face burns a little. So I'm not a fan favorite after all. If what Barry says is even true. Who knows? This is television.

Mariah and Giselle hug each other and move closer to Blitz.

Barry looks over all of us with a dramatic pause. "And the third girl who gets to stay another week is..."

Another pause. A musical pulse plays in the silence, like a heartbeat.

"Livia Mays!"

I let out a breath and hug Christy. Then I step over next to Mariah and Giselle.

Christy starts crying. Blitz comes up to her and brushes a tear off her cheek.

Barry says, "That means Christy will not be back

on *Dance Blitz*. She and Blitz Craven will do their final dance together tonight for all of her fans."

Mariah, Giselle, and I head offstage. We're done for the night.

I turn to watch Christy dance with Blitz. It's nothing fancy, just a tight slow dance. She is crying hard. Blitz pats her back and pays close attention, murmuring things in her ear.

"Another week, another paycheck," Giselle says as she passes by me to head to the hall. "Expect next week to get a lot crazier."

Now that the show is over, I'm dying to know if they aired the lunch clip. I follow Mariah out into the hall.

"Did they show the lunch footage?" I ask her. "I couldn't bear to watch."

"Yeah," she says. "They showed Giselle's meltdown. It was all geared to make her look dramatic. She's getting a lot of airtime."

"She makes good Tweets," I say, then bite my lip as I realize I've made a gaffe. Blitz's Tweet is what got us in this whole mess.

Mariah shrugs. "I'm just glad they kept me in a good light. I'm not after a career in television. Just dance."

"You were really great in rehearsal with that instructor. You two are an amazing fit."

She pauses at that, looking thoughtful. "Yes, it

does seem easier with him. But he's not a career-maker. Blitz is."

"So that's all they did of the lunch?" I ask.

"If you're worried about what you said, it's probably too much for television. But I expect if ratings aren't up this week, it will get leaked."

This shocks me. "Who would leak it?"

"Oh, they have their ways," Mariah says. "Have a good night." She heads off for her dressing room.

Cast and crew start streaming out of the backstage, so I know the show is over. I head to my own room to get out of the makeup and this darned tutu.

Chapter Thirty-Two

T he sexy dance show scares the crap out of me, honestly. It's three days away and Blitz hasn't rehearsed with me yet, so the dance trainer standing in has to do all the moves, his hands all over my body, the near kisses. I'm not professional at all about it, uptight, anxious, and stiff.

Now that we're so close to episode four, Amara comes to the rehearsals herself. "This is horrible," she says. "We have to get Blitz in here."

Apparently Mariah is having more trouble than I am, so he's been practicing extra with her. But within a half hour, he's in the studio.

"I finally get to be sexy with you," he says. His hair is all over the place.

"Is part of your Mariah dance that she musses your hair?" I ask.

Blitz shakes his head. "Blame Giselle for that. They're filming all sorts of stupidity in the dressing rooms between rehearsals."

They aren't doing that with me. I feel worse than ever, imagining what she is doing, and how little she is probably wearing when she does it.

"Don't worry," Blitz says. "She's playing the tramp card for a reason. She's got her sights on some upcoming TV drama that is being cast, and she wants as much airtime as she can scrounge."

"All they have done with me is rehearsal footage and interviews," I say.

"Oh, it's coming," he says. "Your assistant Jessie will get a new schedule today. Shelly told me you and I were going to be filmed at an aerial silk studio and it was supposed to get very friendly."

Oh my God. My voice shakes as I ask, "They're going to run the lunch clip, then?"

"Not sure if it will go on air," he says. "They won't tell me. But there will be something about it."

The dance coach starts the music. "We're going to show you the dance," he tells Blitz. "You will pick it up very easily. Feel free to improvise."

God, Blitz watching me do this thing with someone else is a thousand times worse. I stumble twice, miss a lift, and find myself squeezing my eyes shut when he runs his hands down my dance outfit.

Finally, it's over.

"You really are only good with Blitz, aren't you?" Amara observes.

Why can't the cameras be here when she says stuff like that?

"I've got the idea," Blitz says. "Let's not torture her anymore. Just talk me through it."

We work, movement by movement, through the number. As always, Blitz learns quickly, first getting the basics, then adding finesse and flair. By the end of an hour, we have a rough working dance.

"We're good with her for the day," Amara says. "We'll hit it again tomorrow."

Shelly pops her head in. "Blitz, Studio B for Giselle in five."

Gah. Her again.

I turn to Jessie, who is sitting in the corner with my bag. "What do I have next?" I ask her.

She pulls out the paper schedule. "Just says dance block," she says. "Then a costume fitting in an hour."

I wait for Amara and Blitz to leave, then ask the dance coach if we're good for today.

"Sure," he says. "You do much better with Blitz anyway."

"This dance is hard for me," I say, heading for the door. I wave for Jessie to follow.

"Where are we going?" she asks.

"Studio B," I say. "I want to know if there are cameras."

Jessie follows as I hurry down the hall. If I see anyone, I might lose my nerve.

The windows to the studios are very small, only six inches wide. I peer in, and catch a glimpse of Blitz and Giselle in the mirror before they are out of range of my limited vision.

I take a deep breath and open the door.

The music is a blues number with a sultry low female voice. Blitz has Giselle bent over his arm and leans over her, his face lowering closer and closer, before she turns him aside in a dramatic rejection.

They've had him take off his shirt for this rehearsal, so he wears only the form-fitted dance shorts.

Amara looks up, but doesn't want to disturb the dance, so she says nothing.

And there is a camera. In the corner, one of the crew members squats down, holding a rig.

Why are they filming Giselle with Blitz but not me?

I swear they want her to win. Maybe she's made some behind-the-scene deal. Maybe all the voting is just for show, and it doesn't count.

My stomach turns over.

The dance is arresting. Giselle rolls out of reach and Blitz is on the ground tumbling toward her and bracketing her body with his.

Giselle wears a skin-colored body suit, so when he

does this, a quick glance would suggest she is naked. With his bare chest, this footage could look like anything.

I want to go over there, break it up, call everyone out on what they are doing. But I don't. I just stand there like an ice statue, unmoving, barely breathing.

Giselle's legs come up and around Blitz's body, and they roll together this time. Blitz notices me and stops abruptly. Giselle keeps rolling and ends up alone at the end of the mat.

"What the hell?" she says.

"Hey, baby, everything okay?" Blitz asks.

I look at him, and Giselle, then Amara and the camera. "Who decides what is filmed?" I ask. "Who chooses the clips?"

"Devon, honey," Amara says. "He's the director. If you feel you're getting shortchanged, take it up with him." She walks me to the door. "This session is closed."

I turn back to Blitz. He's not happy about Amara escorting me out.

"I'll come find you as soon as we're done here," Blitz says.

But he doesn't insist on them letting me stay.

I don't know where to go. I won't talk to Devon, of course not. But I don't want to go in my dressing room where there are cameras. Or any room, really.

They could be anywhere, waiting to film me looking dejected and angry.

The safest place is the hall. Or maybe the parking lot. I leave Jessie in the viewing room to hang out with the other assistants who are waiting to be called on, and walk outside.

It's a gorgeous day, typical Southern California, and I just walk and walk. Some of the studio buildings are quiet, and others are bustling with people, crews, vans of equipment, and props moving back and forth.

I wonder if I can go in any of them, but most of them are keyed, like ours, so I doubt I have access. In fact, I can't even get in ours unless I call Jessie. And she has my phone.

Locked out. It's fine. I wander some more, sitting for a while on a park bench prop by a couple of fake trees. It's fun, feeling like I'm in the middle of television magic. People work their whole lives to be exactly where I am, and never get here.

They get injured, like Jessie, or give up or just never get their chance. I need to see the good side of all this. Have fun with it. Blitz and I are secure. I shouldn't worry about the show. Blitz and I are more than a few dances, bigger than some misleading footage or an audience vote.

I have to have faith.

The giant tower clock on the central building tells me I need to figure out how to get back in the building. Fortunately, the camera crew is packing a van outside the door, and I walk in with them.

Time to do a dress fitting and get my sexy on.

Chapter Thirty-Three

T he fourth show brings a new level of anxiety for me. It's the last elimination and I don't feel I can bring the sexy out in front of an audience.

I'm last in tonight's lineup. I don't know if that's good or bad. Someone has already been eliminated from the show, but nobody knows who.

Mariah seems to have the least footage from the week, looking at Blitz's schedule, plus she was having trouble with her number. So I wonder if the people who know have already stopped pushing her, since it's pointless. From a pure ratings standpoint, the last two people standing should really be me and Giselle. Based on what I've seen filmed, that seems to be what they are going for.

They open with Giselle. I know they want to start strong with a sexy show. She comes before anything else, no clips, no montages, just her and Blitz, rolling on the floor.

The format shifts a little. Barry has an interview set this time, three stools and a wide-screen TV just above and behind them. He runs clips for Blitz and Giselle to comment on.

During rehearsal for this, I was warned that some of the clips and questions would be practiced, but at least one clip and question would be a surprise. The footage I saw earlier that day didn't include any of the lunch conversation. It was typical stuff, an interview about my feelings for Blitz, how I felt about getting this far, and a clip from the previous week's ballet.

So they are going to hit me with something. I'm trying not to worry.

The runner comes for me shortly before my number. I stand up and arrange the outfit carefully.

It's nothing like anything I would ever wear. They continued the royalty theme, with the base being a blue sparkling dress. But it's been destroyed, parts of it ripped, other parts singed on the edges. Over half of it is melted away. I look like a princess from a dystopian land.

Which, I guess, I am.

The tears and ragged edges have to fall just right. Even though there are flesh-colored pieces inside the holes, so I can't accidentally get exposed on live television if something shifts, there isn't a lot of dress left.

My hair is wild. It's meant to get in my face, and for Blitz to push it back. Cecilia back-combed the curls so it's an enormous mass flowing down my back. It's wild enough that we're taking a commercial break between my dance and my interview for the stylist to check me before we do the interview.

The makeup is intense, smoky eyes and vivid lips. I've never looked like this. Blitz saw the dress earlier, but not the hair and makeup. I don't know what he'll think.

Our rehearsals yesterday and this morning were so intense that we struggled to make it home before engaging in fierce, powerful sex. If it weren't for the threat of the cameras, we would have totally done it at the studio.

I feel like a walking nymphomaniac, constantly thinking about the dance, the music, and the heightened emotion of what we've done. It's like a drug.

Jessie follows me and the crew member to the backstage area. As usual, Kendra is there to double-check my look. "You are going to wow them this time," she says.

"It's definitely different," I say.

"Be a Renaissance woman." She turns to the dance coach. "Is she ready?"

"They are going to set the stage on fire," he says.

And with that, we head into the backstage area.

Mariah and Blitz are doing their interview. I can see their legs on the stools even from the far stage wing.

"And what about this move?" Barry asks. "Do legs really spread that wide?"

That gets a whoop from the audience.

They talk about the dance they just did, and I realize the "surprise" footage is rapidly recycled footage from the live dance. Of course. I relax. This will be fine.

The lights go down and Blitz and Mariah head across the stage. Blitz dashes ahead, squeezing my arm as he passes. He can't see me well in this light, so I'm still going to be a surprise.

The commercial begins. I'm about to go into place, when a crew member holds my arm. "You can wait. There's an entire short feature about to run before your number," she says. "You'll go out at the next commercial break."

What? A whole feature?

I can't see the screens at all, but I can hear the sound. Right now, there's just general audience noise as they wait. The crew has already reset the stage during the interview, so all is quiet.

Then the theme music, and Barry's back.

"After tonight, only two girls will remain to claim Blitz's heart," he says. "Earlier in this broadcast, you got to see a behind-the-scenes look at the rather spicy love affair our wayward dance bachelor has conducted with Giselle."

He pauses to let that sink in, or maybe there's a clip running.

"Tonight, in our Sex Blitz episode, you'll see that our sweet girl-next-door Livia has a naughty side as well."

Oh God. They didn't run the footage for the interview because they are going to run it here.

But it's not. Instead, I hear the dance coach talking. "Blitz, slide her into the perfect splits."

I can picture this. It was a rehearsal two days ago, the sexy dance. Blitz and I were pretty feverish. And I remember this moment, because as soon as Blitz got me in the splits, he jokingly pressed his face between my thighs.

I know when that part airs, because the audience cheers and whistles.

I back away from the stage and breathe in and out, concentrating on the sound and expansion of my chest. Barry talks more, but I don't hear him. We knew cameras were there. When I signed up for this show, I told myself I had to stop being afraid, and just do what needed to be done.

But my parents. My church. What if the little dancers from Dreamcatcher saw it? Would Gwen's mother allow Gabriella to watch us? Had she seen and been shocked? Would she never want to do private lessons again?

My father's words come back to me. "You are easily swayed, Livia. You can't be exposed to things that lead you to wicked ways."

This is wicked. This is exactly what he meant. I'm not just being swayed. I'm the one doing the swaying.

A crew member touches my arm. "We're in commercial. Time to go out."

I can't move. I'm paralyzed by my fear, by the repercussions of what I'm doing here.

"It's time," the crew member says again. He looks around, as if he needs help.

Blitz arrives. "You okay, Livia?" he asks.

For a moment I don't answer. I can't speak, that same cold dread coming over me as when we were at the premiere.

He pulls me close. "You're all right. Remember, it's just you and me."

He leads me out, and this time I'm able to move. "You will be spectacular," he says. "Because that's who you always have been."

I want to believe him. I want to feel all right. I have walked away from my past. And my father was wrong. I am not weak, not easily led astray.

I am strong. And he will not shame me.

I stand in our marked spot, waiting for Blitz to grab my waist.

He doesn't talk anymore, just wraps his sure arm around me. He's shirtless in this scene, and with as little as I'm wearing, my skin connects with his. This grounds me. His body. Mine.

Blitz belongs to me, and I to him. His body is mine. His ardor. His love. His sex. This is healthy and part of who we are.

I'm not my father's daughter.

I'm my lover's love.

_*´`*_

WHEN WE HIT OUR LAST POSE, THE AUDIENCE IS ON their feet. They were given paper fans to cool themselves off, a little joke to draw attention to the heat level of the show, and everyone is fanning each other. I can see the white movements even with the glaring lights.

When we go to commercial, Blitz has to help me out of the pretzel-like position. I feel wrung out, like I've run a marathon.

Kendra runs out to check my hair, spraying it away from my face and patting it down. Then she dashes off again. We head over to Barry's stools.

Barry has snatched one of the fans and is waving it at his face when the lights come up. "Whew!" he says. "Is it hot in here?"

My breathing has barely slowed down. Blitz takes my hand. He lifts it as if he's going to kiss it, our signature move, back from our private days and one that has become ours on the show. The fan site has sold thousands of the "Kiss my fingers" T-shirts.

But he bites me instead.

I don't smile, just look at him. Our eyes meet and I feel very powerful, like I'm not the frightened young girl anymore, and this man, regardless of his position, is at my mercy.

He sees it and tilts his head.

"Look at these two," Barry says. "I think we know what's happening after the show!"

Another roar from the crowd.

The video flashes on behind us. As I was warned, there isn't footage I expect, but one from the dance practice with Blitz and Giselle. It shows all of us, then zooms in on me, angry, my eyebrows raised.

Then it freezes.

"Now that's a woman who isn't going to let anybody take her man," Barry says.

Blitz lifts my hand automatically, then catches himself, shrugs, and this time, kisses it. "I love this woman," he says. "Doesn't matter who you vote for."

The crowd goes nuts.

"Well, let's see what America thinks," Barry says. He gestures to the center stage, where Giselle and Mariah are walking out.

Blitz and I leave our stools to go stand in place. This time, despite our instructions, none of the girls hold hands. Both Giselle and Mariah seem really stiff and angry. I guess they heard what Blitz said.

But it's not as if they didn't know.

We wait for Barry to do his theatrics. I watch Blitz. He seems annoyed that he's still not wearing a shirt. I sense that he's getting done with all this too. At least this is the last elimination.

"We have one safe girl who will definitely be back next week," Barry says. "And that is…"

He looks around the audience to buy some time to add to the suspense.

"Mariah!"

Both Giselle and I look at her with shock. We didn't see that coming.

She gets hugs from both of us and stands next to Blitz.

"And our other girl remaining on the show this week is…"

The heartbeat music comes on again, a soft chime pulsing through the room.

"Livia!"

I turn to hug Giselle, but her mouth is wide open.

"What?" she shouts. "That's ridiculous! I'm the best thing on this show!"

Barry keeps a completely straight face as he says, "Apparently not."

I move next to Blitz, mostly to get away from her. Anger is coming off her like a heat wave.

"It's time for Giselle's farewell dance with Blitz," Barry says.

Mariah and I start to walk offstage, but I hesitate. Giselle is not going up to Blitz. She's off script.

"I am not going to dance with that fucking asshole!" she shouts.

I sense a scramble in the back, some shouts to crew. I guess they're going to have to scrub the footage during the slight delay before it broadcasts.

Giselle is not done. "You fucking crucified me, trolled me, and now you think you can get me off your show?" She pushes Blitz in the chest.

"Folks, this is a little off the plan tonight," Barry says.

"Giselle, I don't even know how that Tweet got out," Blitz says. "I would never have done that."

"This is my big fucking break," she says. "And you wrecked it."

"America cast their vote," Barry says, his voice still in announcer mode.

"Then America fucking sucks!" she says.

"And with that, let's have a commercial break," Barry says.

As soon as the feed is cut, two burly crew members come onstage.

"Don't grab me," Giselle says. "I'll take myself out of here."

Blitz goes to her and wraps her in an embrace that makes me have to steel myself. But I can't leave. I'm not sure what's going to happen. So Mariah and I stay near the edge of the stage.

Blitz pulls away from Giselle and looks her straight in the face. I can see he's loading up his charming playboy act. "You're going to take away my last dance? I sure hate to miss that. And I don't want anything to cost you that legal drama you are angling for. Show everyone you're a pro."

This gets her. She breathes fast, out her nose. "I was promised I would be one of the final two."

"It was a legit vote," Blitz says. "None of us have anything to do with it."

"Right," Giselle says. "And pigs fucking fly. We all know everyone's voting for Livia."

I look out in the studio audience. A sea of rectangle lights in the seats means people are videoing this left and right. They should have put the phones in locked storage. Some shows do that now, I hear, to stop illegal videos. This is going to go viral if nobody stops her.

I'm about to go out there myself, but Mariah holds me back. "Let them handle it," she says. "After next week, this whole thing is over."

She's right. What does it matter what Giselle says?

But she's a risk now for the live broadcast. Without a microphone, I doubt any of the phone footage picked up what she was saying. "You think she's right?" I ask Mariah. "Did they bother to use the vote?"

She shrugs. "There is no way to know."

Devon approaches us. "New plan. No dance. We have four minutes to kill. Let's do some individual backstage interviews, one with each of you. Go."

Mariah and I are separated by crew members and hurried to our dressing rooms.

Inside mine, a cameraman is setting up as fast as he can.

An assistant director stands next to him, tapping on his tablet. "Coming up on the end of the break," he says.

I start to panic as he starts a countdown. I'm all alone in here!

"And in five, four..."

Barry walks in, and I sigh in relief.

"Three, two, one."

The camera turns to Barry. "We're backstage with one of our two final girls in this crazy episode of *Dance Blitz*." He turns to me. "Livia, how surprised are you to be one of the last girls standing?"

Ugh. What a question. If I say I expected it, I'm

egotistical. If I say I didn't, it suggests I don't have a special connection with Blitz.

"Any ideas?" Barry prompts. "What did you think of tonight?"

I wonder — what would Blitz do? And I have it.

"It's all about the fans," I say. "They had faith in me, and I am so grateful."

Barry turns to the camera. "Isn't she a doll, America? Don't forget to vote on your choice tonight! You have two hours after the broadcast to get it in."

Back to me. "Livia, if you had one thing to say that would sway the viewers out there to cast their vote for you, what would it be?"

That's simple. "I'm the one who truly loves him."

Barry puts his hand over his heart. "Our director is still onstage with Blitz, where they're recovering from Giselle's crazy train. Let's see what is in our dancing Romeo's mind now that he's missed his last dance with the wild, passionate Giselle."

The camera light goes off. "Thanks, Livia," Barry says. He and the cameraman hurry out into the hall, probably to go see Mariah in her room.

I lay my head on the counter as Jessie rushes in.

"Oh my God, Livia, what happened to Giselle? Is she crazy? She dropped like five thousand f-bombs on live television!"

My head twists so I can look at her. "There's a

thirty-second delay so they can bleep it out before it actually goes live."

"Oh, thank God," Jessie says, collapsing in a chair. "I thought they were going to have to carry her off the stage."

"They don't like wild cards on live TV," I say.

"I guess this is it," Jessie says. "The episode tonight determines the votes for the last show. What are you guys going to do on it?"

"They are bringing back a bunch of the girls for group numbers," I say. "I'll have a dance with Blitz, and Mariah will have one, and we will take part in a silly one where they are all fighting over him."

"Oh, that sounds fun," she says.

The noise level outside intensifies, indicating the live show is over. Jessie opens the door. "See you on Thursday," she says.

"Bye, Jessie."

I realize I only have one more week with her, with all this. I've gotten to know more people in the past couple of months than in the past four years. A lump forms in my throat. I won't miss the drama and the crazy schedule and the other finalists. But going back to normal life will definitely be a change.

Chapter Thirty-Four

Giselle's meltdown is something Blitz and I don't talk about much. Despite our difficulties with her, neither of us like how things ended. We speculate that maybe she thought she was going to get special treatment due to her relationship with a producer, or maybe it was even promised.

But we don't know. Even Blitz isn't privy to that level of internal deception if it were true.

The last week of rehearsals is very different from the others. Twenty former *Dance Blitz* contestants return, including the finalists from season one, when Blitz refused to accept any of them.

There are only five dressing rooms other than Blitz's, so we all end up sharing. Three girls from season two come to mine, and immediately they laugh when they see I've covered up the mirror.

"I did that too!" exclaims a friendly Hispanic girl with a wild curly mane of hair. "But you missed this one!" She tugs on the baseplate below one of the mirror lights and it swings open. Another camera points at the door.

"Oh!" I say. "Is that all?"

"That's all we knew about," she says, and introduces herself as Amelia. "One of our girls was so paranoid she draped all the walls with sheets."

"And you came back for more this week," I say.

"You bet we did!" Amelia says, turning to the mirror to pick out some of her curls. "There is no better exposure for getting new work than to go on one of these reality shows. I've been trying to get on *Dancing with the Stars* as a trainer partner for a year!"

One of the crew girls pops her head in. "Dance rehearsal onstage in five," she says.

We head out into the hall to go to the main stage. This last episode is just for fun until the winner is announced, as the votes were already tallied the previous week. So there will be upbeat numbers, clips from both seasons, and interviews to close out the show.

Blitz is already onstage when we get there, and he gets caught up in the sea of girls who want to hug him or just get close. I hang back, and I catch Mariah doing the same. She seems particularly interested in watching some of the other second-season girls and how they interact with him.

I wonder what she thinks will happen even if she wins. He's just going to do his final dance with her, say good-bye to everyone, and move on.

Amara claps her hands to quiet everyone. "All right, girls, we have four instructors here to help you all. This number is designed to spotlight each of you for a few seconds. About halfway in, Blitz will arrive, then near the end, Mariah and Livia. Let's get everyone in a starting position."

The rehearsal is way more lively than anything we've done before. None of the practice studios will hold us all, so we stay on the stage much of the day.

In addition to the big opening scene, some of the girls have their own numbers with guest dancers to fill out the male roles. Blitz will only dance onstage in the opener, then two spotlights on me and Mariah.

For our last dance, Blitz and I are doing aerial silks. It was a natural fit after all the talk about them. It has a circus feel, a little on the silly side, and we'll do some fun drops that will make the audience gasp. They look way harder than they are.

While the main girls work out their parts, Blitz, Mariah, and I sit out in the audience. Blitz tells me about some of the girls, and he and Mariah particularly enjoy sharing stories about some of the recent ones.

I'm already feeling nostalgic by the time the day ends. There's only three days left of rehearsals with everyone, and the show.

Then it will be over.

Chapter Thirty-Five

A live show with this many girls is an entirely different animal than the ones with only finalists. The halls are often filled with people, girls in their costumes, small prop tables, and extra crew. I get the idea that this is what the early parts of each season were like, as everyone seems familiar with the setup.

Backstage has to be controlled, as all the girls want to watch everything and it's too hectic, plus the noise level is too much for a live show. Duke ends up doing some security work keeping the girls corralled and out of the stage wings.

Watching his eyes light on one scantily clad dancer after another, it's clear that he does not mind.

The show begins with a bit where Barry shows clips of some of the highlights of the show. The girls are all rapt, watching for mentions of themselves on the screen in the dressing room.

After a few minutes of that, I decide to wander down to Blitz's dressing room. I'd rather spend the last few minutes before our final show with him.

A hulking man in the crew's black outfits stands outside Blitz's door, presumably to keep the girls out. As far as I know, they aren't doing any live bits anywhere beyond the stage. All the clips were prerecorded.

He looks at me as I approach, and I think he'll keep me out, but he doesn't. His meaty hand opens the door. "Good evening, Miss Livia," he says.

Shelly is inside with Blitz, as well as a wardrobe girl. They arrange all his costumes in order.

Blitz is lying on a bench by the back wall, his forearm across his face.

"Is this a preshow ritual I don't know about?" I ask.

He moves aside and smiles when he sees me. "You have entered the den of iniquity!" he says.

I look around. "The camera-filled den," I say. "Between me and the girls, we've got all the ones in our dressing room covered up."

"They won't allow me to do that," he says, sitting up and patting the cushioned bench beside him. "But we should be done with them. I don't think there will be any surprises tonight other than the winner."

I sit down next to him. I'm in a sparkly royal-blue dress, very traditional for dance, with a fitted top and short skirt. All the girls are wearing the same type of dress for the opening number. Mariah's is emerald green, the color they have always favored for her. Blitz's fitted body suit is half blue, half green. It's all designed so you can pick the three of us out easily. Most of the other girls are wearing subdued colors, pale pink, yellow, peach, mint.

Blitz reaches for my hand and runs his thumb across my palm. He seems nostalgic, and maybe even a little sad.

"Hard to let your show go?" I ask.

He shrugs. "Technically, I let it go when you came on the finale last December," he says. "It was such a shocking end, though, I guess I sailed right through it."

"But not this time," I say.

Shelly and the wardrobe girl discreetly step out of the room.

Blitz draws me closer. "This show made me a household name," he says. "I'm not sad to leave it behind, but it's still a sentimental moment." He glances up at his TV screen, in commercial now, the sound muted. "I like to think it was a success because of me."

"Of course it was," I say. "You're the Blitz of *Dance Blitz*!"

"It's going to go on without me," he says. "They are going to cast a new bachelor for next season."

"You okay with that?" I ask.

"Hell, yeah," he says. "I'm on as a producer. It will be a steady income long after I'm gone."

"When did this happen?"

"Earlier today. Signed provisional agreements."

"Will you need to be in LA?"

"Not at all," he says. "No more than Bennett is."

"Is he still a producer?" I ask.

"Nope. Sold me his share."

I lay my head against his shoulder, realize I'm crushing my hair, and sit up again. "Tomorrow we get to go back to real life," I say.

"We do. I thought we could hang out another week or so in the LA place, then fly back."

"Sounds good to me," I say.

Shelly pops her head in. "Time for the opening number," she says.

We get up, fingers still entangled, to head to our final moments on the stage.

Chapter Thirty-Six

ᴥᴥᴥ

One girl falls during her dance, which creates a little drama for the show when she has to be carried off. It also runs us behind, and a few clips have to be cut to keep us on track. My dance with Blitz goes well, as does Mariah's. There's a lot of laughter and a party atmosphere in the halls.

By the time all the girls line up in a giant semi-circle at the back of the stage for the announcement of the winner, everyone is more subdued. It's an ending for Blitz, and everyone seems to be thinking about the dreams that were dashed here when they weren't chosen.

I'm deadly calm. I know where my life is going, starting tomorrow. What the viewers do for the vote is really irrelevant.

Mariah, too, seems relaxed. She smiles at me as

we take our places on the stage. Blitz holds a giant bouquet of flowers. There will be no farewell dance tonight, only one with the winner.

It's the same dance we prepared in the event of a farewell earlier in the season, nothing dramatic. It's my understanding that confetti is going to fall, and that the audience members in the seats will be dropped T-shirts and other swag after the announcement. Apparently a few vendors have known all week who the winner was, but nobody has leaked it.

Barry is dramatic, as always. I watch him talk, savoring this last moment of seeing him right in front of me, working the audience in his smooth announcer way. I assume he'll get to stay as the new bachelor arrives. I think of some other man on the stage, wooing a new set of girls. I'll have to ask Blitz if it's going to be live or recorded, the dancer's choice or a viewer vote.

But that doesn't matter right now.

Beyond the stage lights, in the parts I can see despite the glare, are the audience members. It's different from that first fledgling recital I did years ago at Dreamcatcher Academy, but in a lot of ways it's the same. I've done my best, held up against nervousness and fear. I got it done.

The giant screens are focused on me and Mariah. Barry turns and looks at Blitz. I no longer really register what he's saying, just take in the moment, the roar of expectation, the excitement in the restless crowd.

"Tonight Blitz gets to tell us the winner," Barry says, and this gets my attention. "He may have given the choice to you, America, but he'll get to say her name."

I wonder if he'd change it, make the winner be who he wants after all. His grin is devilish, possibly imagining what would happen if the girl he hands the flowers to isn't the same as the one on all the T-shirts about to be dropped.

Blitz turns around, his face looking straight into the live camera. "It is my immense pleasure to finally announce the winner of *Dance Blitz*."

He turns to look at the two of us. "They are both great women, and I've been honored to work with them."

He flashes a grin at us both. "But the girl you chose is Livia Mays."

The crowd goes crazy. I watch Blitz's face, earnest and happy. I wonder if I'm the real winner, if the vote counted.

But it doesn't matter.

Mariah gives me a quick hug and quickly exits the stage. Blitz approaches me with the flowers and leans over them to give me a long, lingering kiss.

This is our moment, and as promised, pale

sparkling confetti dots the stage as it rains down from overhead.

The shirts start dropping over the audience, and we pause to watch the fans catch them. On the big screen, a camera zooms in on a fan holding one up. It has a big heart with a picture of me and Blitz.

So it was me.

One of the old contestants comes forward to take the flowers, and everyone backs off to the farthest reaches of the stage.

Our music begins, the song Blitz and I picked out. It could have been a song for a farewell dance, if all the fans out there had chosen to send me home. But they didn't, and all the stars align in this one moment, me, Blitz, our dance, his show, this end.

As he takes me in his arms for the waltz, I know it isn't an end at all. It's just a continuation of what we already knew. That a shy, quiet girl with a love of ballet could fall for the wild, crazy host of a reality TV show.

And it could work.

It already has.

I hope you enjoyed *Wicked Dance*! In the next-to-last book *Tender Dance*, Livia's tenuous relationship with her child is shattered. Lost and distraught, she returns to dance as her solace and lands a part in a major ballet. As both their careers ignite, the couple faces a difficult choice — follow their careers or stay with each other. Get book four or splurge for the entire Lovers Dance Boxed Set.

Also by Deanna Roy

The Forever Series

A young couple reunites in colleges, four years after the death of their newborn.

Book one Forever Innocent *is FREE on all venues.*

- Forever Innocent (Corabelle & Gavin)
- Forever Loved (Corabelle & Gavin)
- Forever Sheltered (Tina & Darion)
- Forever Bound (Jenny & Chance)
- Forever Family (Corabelle, Tina, Jenny)
- Forever Christmas (Corabelle & Gavin)

- Boxed Set: First Three Books
- Boxed Set: Final Three Books

- Stella and Dane (Standalone)

The Lovers Dance Series

A sheltered ballerina is lured into the life of a brash TV reality show star.

- Forbidden Dance
- Wounded Dance
- Wicked Dance
- Tender Dance
- Final Dance

- Lovers Dance Boxed Set

- Billionaire's Dance (a standalone prequel)

Other Books

- Conversations with Little Dude (Nonfiction stories with her son who was adopted from foster care)
- In the Company of Angels (A fill-in-the-pages baby record book for babies lost to miscarriage or stillbirth)
- The Magic Mayhem trilogy of action/adventure books for children ages 9-12.

If you prefer your romances with no graphic love scenes or coarse language

You will love Deanna's pen name Abby Tyler. As Abby, Deanna writes funny, feel-good small-town romances with

a recurring cast of feisty senior citizens and the couples they push together, by hook or by crook.

Deanna is the six-time *USA Today* bestselling author of romance and women's fiction.

She is a passionate advocate for women who have miscarried. She founded the web site Pregnancy-Loss.info in 1998 after the loss of her first baby and continues to run both online and in-person support groups for women who have endured this impossible loss.

She is a foster mom, an adoptive mom, and a baby loss mom. She lives in Austin, Texas, with her family.

Learn more about the author at
www.deannaroy.com

Join her email or text list for new release notices at
Deanna's List

📘 facebook.com/deannaroyauthor

🐦 twitter.com/deannaroy

📷 instagram.com/deannaroyauthor

🅖 goodreads.com/Goodreads

🅱🅱 bookbub.com/authors/deanna-roy

Sneak Peek of Tender Dance

Danika's door is closed, which is very rare. Her office is already isolated on the opposite side of the building from the dance classes. I knock on the solid wood surface.

No one calls out, but after a moment, Danika opens the door. She nods at me. "Hello, Livia," she says. She swings it wide. "Gwen is here."

My daughter's adopted mother has her head in her hands, her elbows braced on the edge of Danika's desk. She doesn't look at me as we all enter.

Blitz stands back in the corner. I take the chair

next to Gwen. Danika settles back in her seat on the opposite side of the desk.

Danika speaks first. "Gwen wants to know if Gabriella is your daughter," she says. "She's the right age, and the resemblance is definitely there."

I glance over at Blitz. He nods. Gwen hasn't changed her position. All I can see is her curly dark brown hair and the curve of her back in a gray sweater.

"Yes," I say. "I gave birth to Gabriella on May 12, 2012. She was six pounds and eight ounces. Fifteen inches long. They tried not to let me see her, but I held her once for a few minutes before they took her away."

"At 8:52 p.m.," Gwen says. "We were downstairs."

"That's what they told me," I say. "The caseworker didn't want me to know if she was a boy or a girl. She was terrible. But I was so scared. I didn't say anything."

Gwen looks up and her eyes meet mine. She looks anguished. "The caseworker *was* awful," she says. "I never liked her, but she brought us our daughter." Her gaze drops. "That was the happiest day of my life."

"It was the worst day of mine," I say simply.

This makes her sit up straight. She looks back at Blitz, then to me. "You're going to take her, aren't you? You have money. Lawyers. You're trying to win her love with these dance lessons so you can have her." She stands up so abruptly that her chair falls back. "Don't you dare! Don't you come near her! Don't you ever look at her again!"

Danika also stands. "Gwen, I assure you, this will be okay."

Gwen turns on her. "What do you know? I've already lost my husband! I can't have children of my own! She will take the only thing that matters to me!" Gwen points at me, her finger an accusation.

"I wouldn't!" I try to say, but it comes out weak and dry.

Gwen stands and hurries for the door. "Don't talk to me!" she says. "I'm hiring a lawyer! Stay away!"

And she's gone.

Danika sinks back down in her chair. She doesn't speak for a moment.

Blitz comes up beside me and wraps his arms around my shoulders. "We have no intention of trying to take Gabriella," he says. "Livia means no harm."

"Harm has been done," Danika says. "Anyone here could connect the dots as well as Gwen has done." She presses the heel of her hand to her forehead. "I think it's best if the two of you take a leave from the academy."

When I make a small strangled sound, Danika looks up sympathetically. "I know it's hard, Livia. I have suspected Gabriella was yours for a while, since that boy came here shouting about your baby. I should have acted on it. I am equally to blame."

"We understand," Blitz says. "Please extend to Gwen, if you get a chance, our regret and that we have no intention of fighting the adoption."

"I'll never see her again," I choke out.

"You've put your name in her files," Blitz says. "She can find you when she is eighteen."

But I can't bear it. May baby is only four.

In Tender Dance, Livia struggles with how to remain in her adopted daughter's life. Lost and distraught, she returns to dance as her solace and lands a part in a major ballet. As both her and Blitz's careers ignite, the couple faces a difficult choice — follow their careers or stay with each other. Get book four or splurge for the entire Lovers Dance Boxed Set.